Rebecca

Ellie's · 2 · People

Books by
Mary Christner Borntrager

Ellie

Rebecca

Rachel

Daniel

Reuben

Andy

Polly

Sarah

Mandy

Annie

Over half a million books in print
in the Ellie's People Series.

This series is available
in regular type and
in large-print type.

Rebecca

Mary Christner Borntrager

HERALD PRESS
Scottdale, Pennsylvania
Waterloo, Ontario

Library of Congress Cataloging-in-Publication Data

Borntrager, Mary Christner, 1921-
    Rebecca / Mary Christner Borntrager.
      p. cm.
    Summary: Becky is torn between her love for a Mennonite
      boy and her loyalty to her parents and the traditions of her
      Amish church.
    ISBN 0-8361-3500-8 (alk. paper)
    ISBN 0-8361-9071-8 (large-print pbk.)
    [1. Amish—Fiction.   2. Mennonites—Fiction.]   1. Title

  PS3552.07544R4 1989
813'.54—dc20   89-32328
[Fic]

The paper used in this publication is recycled and meets the minimum requirements of American National Standard for Information Sciences —Permanence of Paper for Printed Library Materials, ANSI Z39.48-1984.

REBECCA
Copyright © 1989 by Herald Press, Scottdale, Pa. 15683
  Published simultaneously in Canada by Herald Press,
  Waterloo, Ont. N2L 6H7. All rights reserved
Library of Congress Catalog Card Number: 89-32328
International Standard Book Number: 0-8361-3500-8
Printed in the United States of America
Cover art by Edwin Wallace/Book design by Paula M. Johnson
04 03 02 01 00 18 17 16 15 14
103,000 copies in print in all editions

To order or request information, please call
1-800-759-4447 (individuals); 1-800-245-7894 (trade).
Website: www.mph.org

Contents

*In memory
of my late husband, John,
I fondly dedicate this book.*

1

The Powwow Question

It was Monday and Rebecca Eash looked with dread at the stacks of dirty clothes piled on the washhouse floor. She had been working for Emmanuel Lapp's family since April and, by the looks of things, she would probably stay a while yet. Becky liked Amanda Lapp, but why, oh why, did they have such a large family? *Come to think of it,* she mused, *most Amish have big families.*

"Well, one thing sure," she determined, "I am not having more than four children. Two boys and two girls and that's it!" She was a dreamer and an independent girl, this youngest child of David and Ellie Eash. They had brought her up well in accord with the Bible and the Amish faith. But, like her mother at an earlier age, Becky had a mind of her own. Being a good worker, she was much in demand and never wanted for work among her own people.

Bending over, she began sorting the dirty clothes in piles of white only, dozens of diapers, colored things, and the men's heavy work clothes. Then, of course, there were the towels. Towels and washcloths, washcloths and towels. It seemed almost like the words of a song forming in her mind as she worked.

Early that morning Mr. Lapp had carried water to fill the big iron kettle and had built a fire beneath it. By the time Becky cut up the lye soap and dumped it in, the water was almost boiling. She began to sing as she carried pails of hot soapy water and poured them into the washing machine.

"Might as well make the best of it," she said out loud.

"Who are you talking to?" Becky jumped. She had not heard little Sara Lapp come through the door.

"Oh, I was just talking to myself," she answered.

"To yourself. That's funny. I don't talk to myself," remarked Sara.

"Maybe you don't have anything to say," laughed Becky.

"Mom sent me out to help you. She said I can take the clothes from the wringer as you put them through."

"That's good," replied Becky. "Sometimes they get all *ghuddelt* (tangled up)." The washer was filled and now it was time to start the gasoline engine underneath the tub. This Amish home, like all Amish homes, had no electricity. It was an unnecessary convenience.

Becky put her foot on the pedal and pushed down hard. There was only one sputting sound. She tried again. Nothing. Again and again she pushed with quick short pumps, but to no avail.

"I wonder if your dad put gas in here this morning?" she said to Sara. Removing the cap from the small tank, she discovered it was full. Well, that wasn't the problem. She hated to bother any of the menfolk, but had no choice.

"Run to the barn once, *schnell* (quickly), and see if any of the men are still out there. Tell them I can't start the washer." To herself, Becky thought, *I hope Sam was gone to the field already and one of the other boys or Mr. Lapp comes in. Sam is such a tease and makes sheep's eyes at me. I don't care for him at all.* She wished Emmanuel Lapp himself would be the one to come to her aid. The door opened and, much to her dismay, in walked Sam with Sara in tow.

"So you can't start this contraption. What's the problem? Out too late last night with James and didn't get your sleep? So now you are too tired to start a little motor like this. Step aside and let a man handle it."

Oh! Becky wanted to give him a piece of her mind! But she held her tongue as she had been taught to do. In her heart, though, she was thinking, *I hope it won't start. Oh, I hope it won't.*

This time she got her wish.

"What did you do to this engine? I never had trouble with it before. You women always know how to throw a monkey wrench in the works," Sam teased, and then winked at Becky.

She didn't even answer, but turned away and took out a damp cloth to wipe the wire clotheslines.

Sam had to remove the spark plug and clean it before he finally got the motor running.

"That surely couldn't have been my fault," Becky chided, "I never touched the spark plug."

"At least I got it going for you," Sam bragged. "You'd probably still be pushing that pedal. So, it just proves that us men are smarter."

Becky pretended not to hear him and wished he would leave.

"Sam," his sister Sara called to him, "Dad wants you out by the toolshed right away." What a relief this was to Becky.

Becky picked up the first load of clothes and deposited

them in the tub of soapy water. Then, taking a smooth round stick, she poked the clothes so that every last one was immersed completely. This task taken care of, Becky told her little helper she was going to the house to help Amanda until the load of clothes was ready to be put into the rinse water.

"Now, you leave everything alone, Sara," Becky cautioned. "I'll be back soon. Then you can help. Maybe you had better come to the house with me. It could be that the baby needs tending. He has been so *gridlich* (cranky) lately." But little Sara didn't like *gridlich* babies, so she stayed in the washhouse. Just the fact that she had been warned to leave everything alone had aroused Sara's curiosity. Soon she decided the clothes had been scrubbing long enough. Removing the lid from the washer tub, she picked up the stick used to fish out the wet, hot garments. Remembering to stop the agitator, she put the wringer in gear. One by one she wrung out each piece carefully. Then it happened. Several pieces bunched together, stalling the wringer. While untangling them, Sara's hand caught between the rollers. With a jerk they started pulling in her arm up to her elbow.

Upon hearing the screams of the child, Becky came running. No one needed to inform her what had happened. She knew it before she even saw Sara. Why, oh why, had she left her alone by the washer? Quickly Becky released the wringer and then put it in reverse, slowly and carefully removing the little girl's arm. Sara's screaming hadn't lessened and it was piercing to the ears. By now, Mrs. Lapp had come to aid her daughter and the hired girl. She examined the child's arm.

"I don't think it's broken but go at once and send Katie down the road for Franie Marner," Mrs. Lapp told Becky, "She powwows so wonderful good. I think it will be all right."

Becky just stood there for a moment wondering if she had heard right. Surely Amanda Lapp would want a doctor to see Sara's hand and arm. She had heard that some of the Amish believed in this method, but her family never practiced it.

"Well, don't just stand there now. Go, *schnell,* and get Katie." Katie was one of the ten Lapp children. Just a year younger than Sara, she could run like the wind, or so her mother used to say. Perhaps that's why she chose her to run so many errands.

Becky hurried to the springhouse, where Katie was churning butter in the big wooden churn.

"Hurry, Katie, your mom wants you to run to Mrs. Marner's house and tell her to come quick. Sara caught her arm in the washer wringer. Your mom wants Franie to powwow."

"But I don't like to go to her house," Katie informed Becky. "She has a big dog that always barks at me. And Mrs. Marner makes me feel kind of scared. She talks different."

"All I know, Katie, is that your mom said to go fetch her, so you had better go."

Reluctantly, Katie left her churning, ran out the driveway, and turned toward Mrs. Marner's place. Becky returned to the house, thinking perhaps she could help quiet Sara. You could still hear her crying all the way from the springhouse.

"Get me a wet washcloth, Becky," Amanda requested as soon as she spotted her *Maut* (hired girl). And then she made a strange request, "Bring the big family Bible from the living room desk. Franie will be needing it."

Becky wondered about this, but she immediately obeyed.

"Maybe you had better go on with the washing. I think Franie will be here soon," said Amanda.

11

Becky was disappointed. She had so wanted to see what would take place. Never had she seen anyone pow-wow. Well, she was going to ask her mother about it when she would be home for the weekend.

They met just as Becky came through the front gate with a basket full of wet clothes.

"Hello, Becka, how are you tis morning?" said Mrs. Marner. *She does speak different,* Becky thought. *She talks with a lisp.*

"I'm fine," the *Maut* answered politely. "I hope you can help that little girl. She sure has been screaming."

"Dis ish not the firs child I help," stated Mrs. Marner as she continued on toward the house. How Becky would have liked to follow. But she thought it would be better to go on with her work. It wasn't long until she could hear no more cries coming from the house. More surprising yet was the fact that, in fifteen minutes, Sara was back in the washhouse ready to take her place by the rinse tub.

"Oh, Sara, doesn't your arm hurt any more?" asked Becky.

"No, it doesn't," said the little miss.

"But you cried and screamed so. Surely it must have hurt very badly."

"Yeah, it did, but now it doesn't."

"Not one bit?" Becky couldn't believe it.

"Not one bit," answered Sara.

"Well, what did Franie do to make it stop?" pried the hired girl in amazement.

"Oh, she told us all to be real quiet. I wasn't allowed to move. I could hardly stop crying, but she said I had to so she could work. Then she took the big Bible and opened it to about the middle. After that, she put her one hand on the Bible and the other on my arm where it hurt. She looked as if she were talking, but I couldn't hear anything. Next, she took a white handkerchief from her big apron pocket and laid it on my head and said something about a green olive tree. I felt hot all over and then kind of cool. It seemed so tingly and good. She took the handkerchief from my head and asked if my arm still hurt, and it didn't anymore."

"Oh, Sara," was all Becky could say. She sure was going to ask her parents about this.

Becky was very tired when she went upstairs that evening. As was her custom, she took her Bible to read a portion of Scripture before retiring. She loved the Psalms and chose to read from them. Sara, who shared a room with Becky, sat on the bed beside her.

"Do you want me to read out loud again?" she asked her little roommate.

"Yes, I like that," Sara told her.

Becky read Psalm fifty-two. When she came to verse eight, she suddenly suppressed a gasp.

"What's wrong?" asked Sara, "Why did you stop?"

For a brief moment, Becky could not answer. For these are the words she was about to read:

But I am like a green olive tree in the house of God:
I trust in the mercy of God for ever and ever.

What could it mean? Had God directed her reading for a special reason? Was this perhaps the verse Franie Marner had used to stop Sara's pain?

"Becky, what's wrong?" Sara again inquired.

All Becky said was, "I'm tired and I don't want to read anymore. Let's go to bed now."

With that done, she blew out the kerosene lamp and climbed in beside her little friend.

For a while she lay trembling in the darkness. *I must tell Susan Miller about this too,* Becky decided. Susan's parents had moved close to the Eash farm two years ago.

They were Mennonite people. Even though the family had many things considered worldly by Amish standards of the 1950s, the Eashes and Millers became good friends. Susan had three brothers and one sister. Often, on Sunday afternoons, the families would visit each other, and, during the week, help with farm work.

Becky knew she would see Susan sometime during the weekend and she must remember to ask her if she had ever seen anyone powwow. Susan knew her Bible well. She went to Bible school and to Young Folk's Literary, so she could explain Psalm fifty-two, verse eight. That's what Becky would do. She was going to ask Susan.

2
A Dating Decision

It seemed good to be home. It was much quieter in the Eash household than at the Lapp's.

"You can't even hear yourself think," Becky told her mother. "If the baby isn't crying, then the toddlers are scrapping or clamoring for attention. And that Sam! I just cannot stand being around him. He is so loud and boisterous. They have strange ways too."

"Slow down once, Becky," Ellie said, "All families are different. Just wait until you have children of your own. You will find out it won't be very quiet at your house, either."

"I'm not having them by the dozen," Becky remarked.

"Rebecca!" remonstrated her mother. She was totally shocked at her daughter's words. "It is not for us to determine such a matter."

Becky didn't answer the rebuke she received, but to herself she vowed she *would* determine it.

After supper, Becky told her folks she would like to go down to Susan Miller's for a while. The Millers lived within walking distance, so the two girls would frequently spend an evening together.

"Oh," said her father, "want to catch up on all the neighborhood news? Well, I've heard say the quickest way to get word of what's happening is telephone, telegraph, and tell a woman."

"Oh, David," said Ellie, "you are just as big a tease as ever. We know that isn't true, don't we, Becky?"

"They sure can *gaxe* (cackle) a lot," David laughingly replied.

"Oh, you!" was all Becky said, cuffing her dad lightly on the arm.

"Don't stay too late, and be sure to take a flashlight," Ellie reminded her daughter.

"All right," Becky said, and she was out the door, flashlight in hand.

Susan Miller was just finishing the supper dishes.

"Becky, come in," she called, spying her friend coming up the porch steps. "Am I glad to see you! I've got lots to tell you. Here, sit down." She drew a chair away from the table for Becky.

"No, no, thank you. I'll help with the dishes so we can have more time to ourselves," Becky responded.

"Okay," Susan replied, handing her friend a towel.

Becky liked visiting with Susan. The Millers had everything so handy, too. Electric lights, a telephone, running water and, best of all, a bathroom. Susan didn't know how lucky she was. Becky often wondered why it was all right for Susan's family and others to have these conveniences, but not for Amish people. She had asked her parents, but they just said, "*Es vor immer so* (it has always been this way)." That answer didn't really satisfy her. She made up her mind to find out why it's always been "*immer so*."

Mrs. Miller came from the living room carrying a

tablecloth she had just finished edging.

"Well, hello, Becky. I thought I heard voices out here. How are your folks?"

"They are fine," Becky said.

"Tell them I said 'Hello' and, if your mother wants to go to the Hershberger auction next Thursday, she can go with me. I'm going anyway and she won't need to bother hitching up the horse. I'll stop by around nine to see if she would like to go along."

"That's nice of you, and I'll tell Mom," Becky replied.

As soon as the girls were finished with the dishes, they went upstairs to Susan's room. It would have been more pleasant sitting on the porch swing, but not as private. And they preferred privacy.

Becky wondered what Susan had to tell her that was so secret. She didn't have long to wait. The girls got settled on Susan's bed and then the suspense was broken.

"Becky," Susan began, "James wants me to find out if you could go to Young Folk's Literary with him next Wednesday night."

"What?" exclaimed Becky. True, she thought James Miller was an attractive fellow and some folks, like Sam Lapp, inferred that she dated him; but she never had. They were just good friends, that was all. Or was it? Her heart was beating so. But it was because of what her parents would say. She was sure that's what caused the pounding in her chest and her flushed, hot face.

"You're blushing," Susan laughed.

"Well—well, I don't know what to do," stammered Becky. "My folks might not like it."

"Why not?" wondered Susan.

"They would rather I'd stay with our own young people."

"What shall I tell my brother, then?" Susan asked. "I wish you could go. Arnie Johns and I are going together and, if the four of us could ride in one car, we would have fun, I know."

Becky did not know who Arnie Johns was, but if he was a friend of Susan, he must be okay. So, without really meaning to, she said she would go.

"But just this once, mind you," she said in response to her friend's squeal of delight.

"I'll tell James then. He can pick you up around seven, if that's all right. We will meet here and all go in Arnie's car when he comes for me. Oh, Becky, it will be a great evening."

"Susan," Becky began, "I have something to ask you. Did you ever watch anyone powwow?"

"No, I never did. Why do you want to know?" inquired her neighbor friend.

Becky then related the whole incident of little Sara Lapp's accident.

"You mean Franie Marner can control pain?" Susan was amazed at what she was hearing. She had heard about this practice, but she was not familiar with it. It sounded rather scary to her. The girls both thought, from what little they heard about Mrs. Marner, that she seemed like a fine person.

"What did your parents think about it, Becky?"

"Oh, I haven't told them yet. But I'm going to. I just thought that you know your Bible so well, maybe you could tell me why she used that verse from Psalm fifty-two."

"I have no idea," answered Susan, "but I'm going to ask my folks, too."

The girls talked until almost nine. Realizing how late it was, Becky said she must be going. She didn't want to worry her mother. Mrs. Eash was quicker to fret if Becky wasn't home exactly on time than was her father. So, thanking her friend for the evening, she said her good-bye and started for home. But not before Susan reminded her about the plans for Wednesday night.

Why, oh why, had she said she would go? But a promise is something not to be broken, she had been taught as a child. She had also been taught to think carefully before making a promise.

Well, she would just have to be more careful hereafter. Becky was glad her mom and dad were not retired for the night yet. Now she would ask them about Mrs. Marner and Sara Lapp's episode.

Taking her shoes off, she leaned back in the comfortable rocker. Her dad looked up from the farm paper he had been reading.

"Vel now," he remarked, "did you learn a lot tonight?"

"No, Dad, I didn't, but I'd like to learn something," his daughter answered.

David Eash looked at her with surprise. Her mother, too, laid aside her mending, sat up, and took notice.

"*Raus mit* (out with it)," her dad said. "What do you want to know?" He fully expected questions such as Becky sometimes asked after spending time with her Mennonite neighbors. Questions about worldly things. This time quite a different conversation would take place.

"Have you ever heard of powwowing?" asked Becky.

"Oh, sure!" David replied. "What makes you so interested in that?"

So Becky told the complete story of all that took place at the Lapp's home when little Sara caught her arm in the washer wringer.

"Oh my," said Ellie, "you mean to tell me that child was not even seen by a doctor? She could have had a broken arm. I don't understand why some people take such chances. I certainly wouldn't—"

"Now, Mom," David interrupted his wife, "not every

19

woman is such a mother hen as you. I mean, you were always so concerned about the children and not—"

"Is that bad?" Now Ellie interrupted her husband.

"Oh no, of course not. But I was just going to say, not every child is so fortunate as ours were." He got himself out of that jam.

"Yes, and people aren't all alike," answered Ellie. That seemed to be one of her favorite reminders whenever she thought someone was critical of others.

"That's for sure," said Becky, "Who ever heard of putting a handkerchief on someone's head and taking a verse from the Bible to stop pain?"

"But you said it did stop."

"Yes, Dad, I did say that. It did stop. Sara came back to the washhouse only about fifteen minutes after Franie went into the house. What does it all mean?"

"To tell you the truth, Becky," Mr. Eash answered, "I don't really know. Some of our people do powwowing for different things. There are those who think it isn't right. Others think it's a gift of healing. The Bible does speak about different gifts and healing is one of them. As for me, I'm just not sure what to make of it."

"Then why don't they just call it a gift of healing instead of powwow? That sounds like some kind of hexing."

"Rebecca!" Ellie said forcefully. She always used her daughter's full name when she meant to reprimand her. "Rebecca, we don't use that word, and we don't judge others. The main thing is, it worked, and little Sara was relieved of her pain. I would suppose if you were in misery like Sara was, you wouldn't care how the cure was done, just so you could get relief."

Becky could not argue with that, but she still thought it strange and hoped within her heart that some day she could observe this ritual being performed.

Becky sat awhile yet. It was so nice to spend a quiet evening with her parents. Should she tell them of her promise to go the Mennonite literary meeting with James Miller? Even though she was twenty-one and her own boss (as the Amish put it), she was still expected to let them know of her whereabouts when she went anywhere. This was a matter of courtesy. She remembered the evening when she had been at the Amish young folks' singing and her Grandma Maust had passed away very suddenly, as had Grandpa earlier. There was no doubt that she would need to tell her parents before next Wednesday night. Maybe she could wait until early Monday morning, just before going back to the Lapp's. That way they did not have as much time to talk about it. If it wasn't wrong to go with James, why did she feel so guilty?

The weekend passed quickly. At Sunday evening singing Becky had three offers of a ride home. She had come earlier with her friend Edna and Edna's older brother. They only lived two miles from the Eash farm. Edna said her brother didn't mind picking her up. Levi was a kind youth, and Becky appreciated him a lot. Sam Lapp was the first who asked to take Becky home. She refused. Because she had not accepted Sam's offer of a way home, she turned down the other two fellows too. For a fleeting moment she thought, *If James Miller were here and asked me, I'd say yes. And I wouldn't care if it seemed fair to the others or not.* Oh, she must not think such thoughts.

Monday morning dawned cloudy and with rain pattering against the window-panes. Not exactly what Becky needed to bolster her courage to break the word to her parents about Wednesday evening. However, at the breakfast table she knew she could wait no longer.

"Mom, Dad," she began, "I have something to tell you.

James Miller asked me to go with him to their young folks' meeting on Wednesday night."

"Surely you told him you wouldn't," Mrs. Eash said. There was only silence.

"Becky," Mr. Eash spoke up now, "answer your mother. What did you tell him?"

"It wasn't really James that asked. He had his sister Susan talk to me about it."

"Oh, so he gets someone else to do his sly work. He knows the Amish people don't want their young boys and girls mingling with his kind."

"What do you mean by 'his kind,' Dad? I thought we were always told to befriend everyone," Becky wanted to know.

"Becky," said her mother, "you know we believe that way. But when it comes to dating, there we draw the line. Next thing, you would want to marry outside of the church. All your brothers and sisters married Amish companions. You know that's our desire for you."

"Oh, Mom and Dad, who ever said anything about getting married? All I did was tell Susan I would go this once to literary meeting with James. Susan and another boy are going with us, so it's just a friendly time."

"So you did say you will go? Rebecca, I hope you mean it when you say only this one time," her father remarked.

She did not answer him, but turning away, she went upstairs to get her suitcase ready for her week at the Lapp's. When she came downstairs, Sam Lapp was already there waiting for her.

This is all I need, she complained to herself, *to ride with Sam and listen to his arrogant talk.*

"Good-bye, Mom and Dad. I'll see you next Saturday."

"Good-bye, Becky," answered her mother, "We will be praying for you."

Mr. Eash didn't say anything.

3
With the Mennonite Youths

Sam thought it strange that Ellie Eash should make such a parting remark to her daughter. He wondered if something was wrong with Becky and tried, in several ways, to get her to talk. Finally, he asked her outright.

"What did your mother mean when she said, 'We'll be praying for you'?"

"Just that," was the only answer she would give him.

"Don't you feel well?" Sam asked.

"Not really."

"Then why are you coming to work? Maybe it spites you that you didn't let me take you home last night. Well, I could have taken any girl I wanted. So just remember, you aren't the only fish in the sea. In fact, Lucy Reno told my sister she wished I would ask to take *her* home." He looked at Becky with that silly grin of his. The nerve of him. Becky gritted her teeth and clenched her fists to keep herself under control.

The rest of the way Becky had to listen to Sam brag about what a good ball player he was, how he got the better of Jonas Stoll at wrestling, and numerous other feats. She was never so glad as when they turned into the driveway of Emmanuel Lapp's place.

As usual, there were loads and loads of clothes to be washed and Amanda Lapp informed Becky that there would be green beans and peas to put up. Fortunately, several of the Lapp children would be sent to the garden to pick the vegetables, so Becky need not do that cumbersome task. She didn't mind the canning.

By lunchtime, she had lines full of clean clothes and white diapers billowing in the cool breeze. The rain had only lasted for a short time.

"I want to sit by Becky," said little Sara as the family gathered around the table for lunch. Becky was just about perfect in the eyes of the little Amish girl.

"You will sit in your regular place," Emmanuel Lapp informed his daughter.

Sara obeyed, but she pouted.

"Sit up straight now and stop your *brutzing* (pouting)," commanded her father. Then they all bowed their heads for a silent prayer, as they did before and after each meal. After prayer, Becky noticed two tears trickling down Sara's cheeks. She saw that the little miss was trying hard not to cry. *What would it matter,* she thought, *if Sara traded places with Katie or Mosie to sit by her?*

"I don't mind if Sara sits beside me," Becky told Mr. Lapp.

"Well, if you are too good for Sam, then I don't think Sara needs your company," Emmanuel said, rather cooly.

"What?" asked Becky, not believing she heard right. "What did you say?"

"From what Sam told me this morning, you thought you were too much to let him take you home from the singing last night. So that's why I sent him to get you this morning. That way you had no other choice. I don't see why you can't just come over here with him every Sunday evening. That would save us a trip Monday mornings and we could get to the fields earlier."

"Mony," Mrs. Lapp was embarrassed. She always called her husband Mony instead of Emmanuel.

Becky was not embarrassed; she was shocked.

"That is not the reason I didn't let Sam take me home last night," she said, flabbergasted. "Two other boys also offered me a ride, but I said no to them."

"See," Sam spoke up, "she thinks she is too much of a goody for any of us Amish boys. But I bet if that outsider were to ask her, she would go at the drop of a hat."

Sam Lapp didn't realize that what he said would make Becky more certain than ever to go with James Miller. She ate very little that noon and the complete mealtime was very strained.

Mrs. Lapp wished her men folk were not so outspoken. She had a good *Maut,* and she didn't want to lose her. True, she had a large family of her own and her daughters were learning to help around the house, but they were all too small yet to do many of the harder tasks.

Seven boys had made their appearance in the Lapp family before the girls began to arrive. Four of the older boys had married and were starting families of their own. They all married Amish girls and the Lapps were well pleased.

"Amanda," Becky approached her employer, "I have plans for Wednesday evening, if it's all right with you. I won't leave until the supper dishes are cleared away and all the other work is done."

"We should work in the garden until dark. Those weeds are getting ahead of us," Mrs. Lapp remarked.

Becky's heart sank. Perhaps she showed her disappointment, because Amanda paused a bit longer and then she said, "You are a good worker and have never asked to have off before, so I guess you can go." She thought it seemed rather odd that her *Maut* asked to leave in the middle of the week.

Unlike her husband and son, Amanda did not question Becky or make any remarks, but went right on with her canning. Becky, too, began ladling hot peas into the jars for Amanda to seal. She was very grateful to this woman for her thoughtfulness.

Immediately after the supper dishes were done on Wednesday evening, Becky washed her face and hands and ran upstairs. She felt excited and yet, rather naughty. Picking out her very nicest dress, she began to change for her date. Becky looked the very picture of her mother, Ellie, when she was twenty-one. As she combed her long hair, the natural waves fell safely into place. Her nose was tilted slightly and gave her a bit of a saucy appearance. Everyone who really knew her, though, would tell you she was a very friendly girl. Her white covering complemented the black hair. The blue-green eyes looked back at her from the mirror on the dresser, and she smiled approval. Her dad teased her about having green cat eyes. If Becky wore blue, her eyes reflected that color. But if she chose to wear green, then her eyes seemed to be more green. Tonight she was wearing a teal blue color. That's what made her smile of approval, because now her eyes weren't exactly blue or green. The pixie in her showed for just a second. Now her dad wouldn't know if her eyes were blue or green. Her train of thought went back to her weekend at home and she felt a twinge of sadness. But not for long.

Sara Lapp came running upstairs and told her, "Becky, there's a boy downstairs who said he came to get you. He's driving a car and is wearing English clothes. I don't think you want to go with him, but Mom said to tell you he is here." Sara was breathless and looked troubled.

The *Maut* just laughed. "It's all right, Sara," she assured the frightened child. "I knew he was coming, and, yes, I do want to go with him."

"Who is he?" Sara wanted to know, "and where is he taking you?"

"His name is James Miller. His family live neighbors to us. We are going with some friends to the Mennonite young peoples' meeting."

"Oh, Becky," was all Sara could say. She thought it very wrong for Becky to go out with a boy who was not Amish. Thus she had been taught. Becky slipped into her shoes and, picking up her Bible, she made her way downstairs with Sara at her heels.

James was standing just inside the screen door in the kitchen—alone. No one had offered him a seat or stayed to talk.

"Hello, James," Becky greeted him, "I hope I didn't keep you waiting long. I didn't hear you drive in."

"No, I didn't wait long. Besides, I'm a little early. Ready?" he asked, opening the screen door. They stepped out into the early evening light, making their way to the car. James opened the car door for Becky and waited until she was seated before closing it. Then, making his way around to the other side, he got in. The windows were rolled down, so he and Becky could not help but hear the remark Sam made as he watched from the shop where he had been mending a harness for his buggy horse.

"Oh, so the goody-goodies are taking Bibles along. Where are you preaching tonight?" he mocked.

"Don't pay any attention to him," Becky told James.

"I wasn't going to," came his reply.

"Sam seems to have a problem and I hardly know what to do sometimes, or just how to take what he says or does," Becky said.

"Maybe we can make it a matter of prayer at our meeting tonight," James replied.

She hadn't thought of that. In fact, in her home and life, as in most Amish homes, prayer is very private. She knew her parents prayed and she did too, but it was generally in silence. Oh, her dad would read from the prayer book. But as far as audibly praying for a person, she never heard it done.

Their conversation soon turned to various things of the day, and then James said, "Susan tells me Mrs. Marner powwowed for one of Emmanuel's children last week. What do you think of something like that? Does it really work?"

"Oh, yes, it worked and the pain stopped. But I don't know what to say," Becky told him.

"Maybe I'll check into it sometime," James commented.

As they moved along, Becky thought of how much more comfortable it was to ride in a car. Her dad used to say a car goes so fast you don't have time to enjoy God's creation. True, but one sure could enjoy a smoother ride. They talked of numerous things, and before Becky knew it, they were passing her own home on their way to the Miller's.

She caught a glimpse of her mother in the garden. For a moment she felt a twinge of guilt. It was pushed to the back of her mind, however, when she heard James say, "Arnie is here already. That's one thing I can say for him. When he comes to see my sister, he is always on time."

Becky laughed. "Susan is a fun girl. I like to be with her."

"We might as well go in for a while," James said as he opened the door for Becky. "If I know Susan, she isn't ready yet. I always tell her she has to get up before breakfast to be ready by evening."

"Sounds as if you like to tease, too," Becky said.

"My dad always says, 'Boys are made to tease and girls are made to giggle,' " James remarked.

James opened the screen door for Becky, and as she walked into the tidy kitchen, she was greeted by Mr. and Mrs. Miller and Arnie Johns. They seemed to be enjoying each other's company and invited the two young folks to join them.

"My, you look nice tonight, Becky," Mrs. Miller informed her neighbor. Becky blushed, but managed a shy thank you. An Amish girl was not supposed to receive such compliments. It led to *Hochmut* (pride). Nevertheless, it gave Becky a good warm feeling.

When Susan came downstairs, Becky stared at her in admiration. She was wearing a pale yellow dress with a bright yellow daisy print. The young Amish girl thought it was the most beautiful dress she had ever seen. How she wished she would be allowed to wear prints. Her dresses had to be plain colors and all were homemade, usually with the same simple pattern.

"Let's go," said James. "Want me to drive, Arnie?"

"No, I'll drive this time."

As they started for the door, Susan's mother said, *"Ach* (oh), Susan, where is your Bible? You don't want to forget that!"

"No, I don't. Just a minute, I'll be right down." She ran back upstairs.

"That girl," laughed Mr. Miller. "Sometimes I tell her she would forget her head if it weren't fastened on."

She came running down the stairs, cheeks flushed, and announced, "I'm ready."

"Be careful now and don't come home so late," cautioned Susan's mother.

"All right," James answered for them all. With their good-byes said, they started on their way.

29

Becky was just a little frightened. She did not know what to expect. In her mind, she pictured perhaps fifteen or so young folks getting together for a Scripture reading and singing. Susan had told her there would be refreshments. At the Amish singing, the only refreshment was a pitcher of cold water to help keep throats from becoming dry.

There were at least thirty young folks present and one youth was the leader. He announced who would read Scripture, then he himself led in prayer. After that, the group sang a while. Becky thought she had never heard such singing. It was in four parts. Then the leader had them get into groups for a Bible quiz. This truly frightened Becky. She had never taken part in anything like this before, but she did well and her team won. Afterward refreshments were served as they socialized. Everyone was so friendly.

Becky was almost sorry when it was time to leave.

When James took her back to the Lapp home, he asked her, "Did you enjoy the evening?"

"Yes, very much," Becky said. To herself she thought, *More than you will know.*

"Maybe I can see you again, then," James hinted.

"Maybe," she answered. "But now I'd better go on inside. Good night." And she made her way to the house to relive the joy of the evening.

4
Harvest and Hope

It was wheat-cutting time at the Lapp farm. The Amish do not cut by combine, but by horse-drawn binder. This implement binds the wheat into sheaves, which must then be gathered and set up in shocks. Often after the evening chores and meal, the whole family, down to the tots, made their way to the wheat fields to perform this task. The little ones played by the side of the fields while the rest, including the *Maut*, worked diligently. The wheat was scratchy, and Becky rolled her sleeves down to her wrists to better protect her arms. It was an unusually humid day and so she had turned her sleeves up earlier.

"It's very hot, isn't it?" Mrs. Lapp asked Becky.

"Oh, yes, it sure is. As humid as it is, I won't be surprised if we get a good thundershower, so I know the more shocks we get done, the better."

"That's for sure," Amanda remarked. "The wheat is much better protected in shocks. Otherwise, the rain can destroy a lot of it, and Mony says we need as big a crop as we can get."

Becky liked working with Amanda. The men and boys were on the opposite side of the field. On and on they worked, row after row. Then screams came from the little ones playing near the rail fence. Looking in that direction, one could see something drastic was happening. Mrs. Lapp and Becky ran as fast as they could to aid the crying children. They had come upon a bees' nest in the ground and were helpless to fight them off.

Catching up the baby, Becky ran for the buggy and a large water jug. Mrs. Lapp followed with the three-year-old. The four- and five-year-old frightened girls came screaming along behind. Removing the children's clothes as quickly as possible, they splashed cool water on the little faces and bodies. Some of the bees were still clinging to the clothing and had to be shaken free. Mrs. Lapp and Becky received a number of stings themselves. These feisty little insects didn't sting once and be done with it; they were more like a sewing machine. And oh, did it hurt.

"We must get these children home as soon as possible," Amanda told Becky. *"Mach schnell!* Hurry up and help me get them in the buggy. Look how Rosie's eyes are swelling. *Ach* my, they cry so that it scares old Nell." Nell was the buggy horse. She had been tied to the rail fence. Now she was pricking up her ears and prancing nervously because of all the commotion.

Quickly Becky helped put the children in the buggy, untied Nell, and jumped in beside Mrs. Lapp. Taking the lines, she spared no time in heading for the Lapp place. The women were glad the gate to the field had been left open, so they need not stop. Baby Rosie's crying had turned to choking sounds and her lips were a bluish color.

"Stop by Elam Yutzy's place and call the doctor, Becky," said Mrs. Lapp. "Tell him to hurry and come right away."

The Yutzy family was also Amish, but since they were living on a rented farm and didn't own the house, they were allowed to have a telephone. Other Amish were permitted to use it in emergencies or for practical purposes.

When Mrs. Yutzy heard of their plight, she offered to do the calling to save precious time. Amanda was amazed that Becky was so soon in returning from making her call.

"Did you get the doctor?" she inquired.

"Mrs. Yutzy told me she would call him for us. She said we should just go on home," answered the hired girl.

As they pulled into the driveway, Amanda directed Becky to tie the horse to the hitching post, and as soon as they were in the house, she was to make a soda poultice for the bee stings. The *Maut* put the cool paste on the red spots of the children. She even put some on her own burning stings. It felt soothing indeed.

"Shall I put some on the baby?" she asked the distraught mother. By now the child's eyes were completely closed and her breathing was shallow. Instead of crying, she only made a strange squeaking sound.

"Where is that doctor? Why doesn't he hurry? Oh, I wish Mony were here!" The mother walked the floor with the baby in her arms. She didn't seem to realize that it had only been a short while since they had left the Yutzy home. Hopefully the doctor was in, but even so, he had seven miles from town to the Lapp's.

Becky knew Amanda couldn't be reasonable at a time like this, and she didn't know what to say. The other children were quiet now, but they sensed the urgency in their mother's voice and behavior and knew something was not right.

"Here comes your husband now," Becky told Amanda, as she saw Mr. Lapp and Sara crossing the outer yard.

"What's wrong? What happened?" Mony Lapp asked as soon as he came through the door.

"Beestings," answered his wife, "Oh, Mony, look! The baby is bad off. Do something. *Ach* my!"

Mr. Lapp saw at a glance how serious his small daughter's condition was.

"We called the doctor, or rather, we stopped at Elam Yutzy's and his Mrs. said she would call him," Becky said.

"We can't wait for a doctor here," Mony told her. "Quick, run to the Marner's and tell Franie to come now!"

Becky felt a chill go down her spine, but she didn't hesitate. Mrs. Marner dropped her after-supper work of ironing and, without delay, followed Becky back down the road. She asked a few questions and Becky, although almost out of breath, tried to fill her in on details as well as she could.

"Oh, Franie, please help her," Mrs. Lapp pleaded.

Franie reached out her arms and took the rigid child from her mother. One look and she knew she couldn't help.

They heard the noise of someone driving over the gravel in the lane. What a relief as they saw Doctor Lang get out of his car and hurry up the walk. Mr. Lapp was holding the door for him before he reached the porch steps.

"Hurry, doctor," was all Mony could say. His voice quivered so.

"Could you put her down here on the table for me?" the doctor asked. He checked her heart beat and pulse, but shook his head. By his expression, they knew. "I'm sorry," he said. "Even if I had been here when it happened, I could not have prevented this. She is highly allergic to beestings." Again he said, "I'm sorry."

A low moan escaped the lips of the mother as she picked up her unconscious child and hugged her close.

One last little wavering breath and the spirit took its flight.

Amanda was numb as Mony took their departed baby's form and placed her in her crib. The Doctor again checked for vital signs and pronounced her dead.

Franie Marner led Mrs. Lapp to her rocker and sat by her side in silence.

Becky knew she must take charge of the other children, so she put clean clothes on each of the beesting victims and gave each of them a glass of milk. The doctor had recommended milk in case any of them would have reactions. The milk might cause them to become sick and get rid of the poison. Before long the boys came home. They had shocked wheat until dark.

Sam was the first to come in the house. He had seen a few of the neighbors' rigs in the buggy yard. Before Becky could hush him, he asked in that loud voice of his, "What's going on?" He would have said more, but Becky motioned to him to be quiet, and he saw dismay written all over her face.

"I'd rather your dad tell you. But you may want to clean up before you go on into the living room." The other boys came into the house, too, and Becky told them that, while they washed up, she would tell Mr. Lapp they were home.

The three boys stood quietly and listened as their dad told them what had happened. They, too, were stunned by the suddenness of it all.

The Amish keep the bodies of their departed in the home. So the next few days, many friends and neighbors came to share in the Lapp family's grief. Relatives from other states hired drivers with vans and several families shared expenses for the trip.

The funeral service at the home was followed by burial in a nearby plot. The people remained at the gravesite until the casket was lowered and the grave was closed. It was a traumatic experience for a grown person, let alone a child.

Little Sara Lapp was very upset because of losing her baby sister. That first evening after the funeral, she huddled close to Becky.

"Why did God take my sister away?" she asked Becky after they had gone to bed. "I thought God was kind, but now he let those men put my little sister in that deep hole. They covered her up and I don't see how she can ever get out. She is so little." And Sara began to cry as though her heart would break.

How could the hired girl answer this sobbing child? "God is kind," the *Maut* told her. "You see, he took Baby Rosie to a beautiful place where no bees can ever hurt her again. Oh, Sara, if we could see her now, she would probably be smiling and happy."

"But won't she miss us, and Mom for sure?"

"No, oh no, Sara. She would never want to come back to this earth anymore. Everything is so much nicer where she is now."

"No it isn't. How can it be nice in that box and down in the ground?" Sara disagreed with her friend.

"It's only her little body that's there, Sara, but she really isn't in that body anymore. Her spirit went to live with Jesus."

"What's a spirit?" asked Sara.

"Oh, Sara, you ask me so many questions. At the Mennonite Bible Study we were talking about the spirit and soul of a person. They said that when God made man and woman, he gave of his Spirit to each one, so they became alive."

"Well, the Mennonites are different from our church, so I don't know," responded the young Amish miss. "What is the soul?"

"Ask your mom, Sara, and go to sleep now," the hired

girl said wearily.

"I know what a soul is," Sara began talking again. "I have two of them. They are the bottom of my feet."

Becky was amused at Sara's explanation. Sara didn't know why she laughed, but turned her back and was finally quiet.

Summer sped by. Such busy days they were, too.

Threshing time was always a big event. When it came time to thresh at the Lapps', the women had to prepare a meal for ten hardworking hungry men. The big Rumley tractor and the threshing machine itself belonged to Amos Beachy. He would pull his big outfit from one farm to another until all the wheat and oats were in the bins.

The neighbors helped each other load the sheaves in the field and haul them to the thresher. They believed the old adage that "many hands make light work." So they came with their horses, wagons, hayforks, and hired hands or their own grown sons to help at the Lapp home. The grain was separated and stored in bins, but the straw was blown into a straw shed or a stack for later use as winter bedding for the farm animals. Some of it was also used for filling straw ticks for the beds the family slept in.

A large tin tub of clean cool water was placed under a shade tree for the men to use in washing up as they came for the noon meal. Amanda Lapp and her *Maut* had worked hard too. All morning they were cooking, baking, and frying. A meal for threshers usually consisted of mashed potatoes and gravy, chicken (fresh from the hen house), peas, apple sauce, coleslaw, noodles, pickles, puddings, pie, coffee or tea, and of course bread, butter, apple butter, and jam. All of the food was homegrown or homemade.

Becky had to wait table and she heard more than one remark about the good food. There were two Mennonite men and one English man helping today. She liked to see them work together and enjoy each other's company. It seemed to her it should be this way. Everything was almost perfect until the men and boys left the table.

Sam said in a voice for everyone to hear, "Hey, *Mannsleit* (men), if Becky doesn't think she is too English to ride in a buggy, she could bring us some cold lemonade this afternoon."

Becky turned and walked out of the room.

5
The Thunderstorm

Earlier in the summer, Becky had thought of telling Mrs. Lapp she could only work for her until school starts. But after the loss of Amanda's baby, she just couldn't leave her without a *Maut.* Many a time she saw her wipe tears from her face. So Becky decided to stay indefinitely. She sincerely prayed that God would give her a right attitude toward Sam and grace enough to endure his remarks.

The Amish make almost all the clothes they wear, so there would be plenty of sewing to do before school began. Then, of course, there were the men's winter coats plus many broadfall denim pants and chambray shirts. No zippers were used, only buttons or hook and eyes. To sew these onto the finished garments was evening work, done after outside work ceased.

This is what the womenfolk were busying themselves with one evening. It was very hot outside and thunder could be heard rumbling in the distance. Emmanuel Lapp looked up from the farm paper he was reading.

"Sounds like we are in for a storm. Sara, go out to the shop and tell the boys to close the buggy shed door and also the east barn door."

The boys were sharpening some tools by lantern light and as Sara came through the door, Sam asked, "What are you doing out here? Don't you know it sounds like it might rain? Besides it's dark and the *Butzamann* (boogeyman) may get you," he teased.

"Oh, I don't believe in a *Butzamann*," she answered. "Anyhow, Dad said to tell you boys to close the door to the buggy shed and the east barn door."

"Okay. You run along back to the house," her brother Elmer told her. He didn't tease her like Sam did.

The storm seemed to be longer in coming than the family had anticipated. By nine-thirty, the house was quiet and Becky and Sara were preparing for bed.

"Do you like storms, Becky?" Sara asked.

"To tell you the truth, Sara, I don't. But we can't have sunshine all the time. The flowers and garden things need rain to grow."

"But why can't it rain and not thunder and flash so bright?" inquired the little girl.

"I really don't know. But maybe God sends it to wake us up and make us think how powerful and mighty he is," Becky remarked.

"Well, it wakes me up all right," answered Sara. "I can't even get to sleep when it *dunners* (thunders) so."

"Here," said Becky, "let's sit on the bed and I will read to you from the Bible. That always helps me when I'm upset." Putting one arm around the frightened miss and drawing her close to her side, Becky began to read the twenty-third Psalm. She did not realize what an impression her life was making upon Sara. In church, the Amish services were preached in high German rather than in the Pennsylvania Dutch dialect. Children under-

40

stand very little of what is being said. Becky often read in the English language.

But Sara had a question.

"Why did you read 'The Lord is my shepherd. I shall not want'? Don't you want him?" Sara was serious.

Becky laughed, and yet she was glad Sara voiced her question. "Oh, you dear girl, of course I do. I want the Lord in my life more than anything. It means: I shall not want more than I have. I won't lack anything. He supplies all my needs."

"What's 'supplies' mean?"

"Oh, Sara, you are so full of questions again. But I suppose that's how you learn. It means that he gives me all I need. Now go to sleep," Becky said as she blew out the flame from the kerosene lamp and climbed in beside her little pal.

"Vel, I know some things I want and need," Sara remarked.

"Go to sleep and dream you have them. That's the next best thing."

Becky awoke to the voice of Mr. Lapp calling his boys to come right away. *It can't be morning already,* thought Becky. *I've just fallen asleep.* Then she heard a roar and she was wide awake.

"Hurry, *Buwe* (boys), the barn is on fire!"

Sara was awake, too, and crying and clinging to Becky.

"Let go of me, Sara. I must hurry and I can't walk, let alone get dressed, with you hanging onto me like this."

Sara grabbed her own dress and pulled it over her head. It seemed as if she never would find the sleeves. As she struggled to get her arms through, Becky was having her own problems with the pins for her clothes. If she ever wished for a simple closing with a zipper or buttons, it was now.

"Pins are such a botheration," she said. Neither girl

bothered with more than necessary and went running downstairs in their bare feet.

What a sight greeted them as they stepped onto the front lawn. Flames of fire were already shooting way up in the air and sparks were flying everywhere. Most of the Lapp children were crying. Emmanuel and his boys were shouting instructions while trying to move the animals out of the burning building.

Since it had been such a warm night, most of the livestock had been let out to pasture. Yet, when the storm began, they sought shelter in the safety of the loafing shed. They were frightened and reluctant to be forced out into the storm again. Lightning still flashed, thunder crashed, and rain came down in sheets. Everything was utter confusion.

"Run to the neighbor's, Sam, and tell them to get help. Maybe they can get to a phone and call the fire department," Mony shouted to his son. "Hurry! Go as fast as you can." Sam was already halfway out the shed door before his dad finished speaking.

It took some pounding on the neighbor's door to get results. But once Sam stated what he came for, things began to move fast. Neighbors and friends soon began to come from all directions.

With so much help, the animals were moved to safety. There were some other valuables lost to the raging inferno, for by the time the fire engines came roaring into the driveway, one side of the barn and the roof had fallen.

Mrs. Lapp had gathered her children (all except Sara, who was still clinging to Becky's dress) and was watching helplessly from the porch. Many of her church friends were watching with her and trying to console her.

"Ach, Mandy," Jake Katie spoke up. "A barn can be built again. Just be glad you have all your animals out." (The Amish often use the husband's first name with the wife's name. Thus instead of Mrs. Jake Yoder, it's Jake Katie. This identifies which Katie Yoder, since so many of the Amish have the same name.)

Jake Katie did not realize she was of little comfort to Amanda Lapp right then. All Amanda could think of was the loss of the winter storage of hay, the buggy and work harnesses, the newly stored grain, and, of course, the large barn itself. What a blow it must be to her husband. He had worked so hard all summer.

"We will help you rebuild," the men reassured Mony Lapp.

"Don't worry," said the bishop. "You know the Lord always provides."

"*Ya,*" was all Emmanuel Lapp answered, for his voice was quivering and he found it hard to speak.

"Tomorrow morning my boys and I will be over to help you do your milking. Maybe we can empty your toolshed and use it for a cow barn," his next-door neighbor, Vernon Marner, suggested.

Again, Emmanuel only answered with *ya*. He knew he would not sleep anymore that night. Had he been able to think more clearly, he would probably have told Vernon that he and his boys could manage. Not that he wasn't grateful, but Mony Lapp did not like to be beholden to anyone. However, he did accept Mr. Marner's offer to do the milking.

"Sara, let go of my dress so I can walk," Becky said, pulling the tightly gripped hand loose from her skirt. All this while, every chance she had, little Sara Lapp followed Becky and latched onto her.

"My land," Becky continued, "the thunder has let up and the fire is nothing but smoke and you still carry on so. I know you are afraid, but the danger is past now. Let's go see if we can help your mom." Becky and Sara made their way through the group of women on the

43

porch to where Amanda was with the rest of the little ones. Someone had been thoughtful enough to bring a chair for her and she sat holding her two-year-old on her lap.

"Do you want me to take her?" Becky asked, reaching for the little tot.

"Yes, Becky, and try to get the little ones back to bed. I don't think I can sleep. I want to wait here until Mony comes in." A few girls from the church offered to help Becky try to get the little children settled for the rest of the night. It wasn't easy. So many questions were asked.

"What started the fire?" asked four-year-old Annie.

"Why didn't the animals want to come out of the burning barn?" another one wanted to know.

Then Naomi asked, "If the lightning started the fire, where did it get the matches?" This question brought giggles from Becky and the other girls. But it was only natural that she should ask; they were often warned never to play with matches. Toward morning the children slept.

Mrs. Lapp watched her husband wearily walk toward the house with their two sons and a few neighbors, who stayed after the fire trucks left. *How tired Mony looks,* thought his wife. *He even seems to have aged. I must go to him.* She started down the porch steps and began to tell him that they must be thankful the house and family are safe. But before she could say it, Mony remarked, *"Es waar Gottes Wille* (it was God's will)." And that was not to be questioned.

"I'll make some coffee," Becky offered.

"Yes," Amanda agreed, "we will need to talk and make plans and coffee would be good."

"The boys and I need to wash up and then we will be out. Mom, get the large writing tablet and some pencils and take them out to the kitchen table. We will need to do some figuring. Might as well get started," Emmanuel Lapp reasoned.

Mr. Marner joined Emmanuel, his two boys, and Amanda around the kitchen table.

"If there is any way I can be of help to you, Mony," he said, "I'll be more than glad to do what I can." Becky served coffee and then said if she was no longer needed, she would like to go upstairs and try to get a little rest.

"You go ahead," Amanda told her. "If I need you, I'll call you." She knew she couldn't help with the plans to be made, but neither could she leave her husband's side at such a distressing time.

The men began to discuss the size of the barn and the amount of lumber it would take.

"I just can't afford a barn as big as the one I had. We will need to buy hay and grain, not to mention straw."

"Well now," Mr. Marner began, "don't you worry about that. What are we here for if we can't help a brother in need? I'll help you organize a barn raising and the churches will help with the purchase of hay and other feed for your animals."

The sun was just breaking over the horizon when the men finished their figuring and plans of what must be done. Work must go on and so the day began. No one really felt like breakfast except the younger children. Nevertheless, Becky and Amanda prepared a meal as usual.

Just as they were about ready to return thanks for their food and God's blessings to them, little Annie amused them by saying, "That's the first time that barn burned down. I'm going to hide all the matches so the lightning can't find them."

"Yes," her little sister joined in, "and Dad can use all of our building blocks to help make a new barn."

6
Rivals at the Barn Raising

Two weeks after the fire at the Lapp farm, their place was swarming with people. From every direction they came, even from other states. Some arrived by car, others with vans, and many by horse and buggy.

The foundation had already been laid for the new barn. Early in the morning the truck from Will's Lumber Company had brought all the lumber and other materials. All that lacked was the labor. But not any more. There was enough manpower here to put up a new barn before nightfall, and that's exactly what they planned to do.

Womenfolk came too, bringing kettles full of food and all kinds of pies, cakes, and puddings. The men had a hard day's work ahead of them and, by noon, they would be hungry. The women liked to see to it that they were well-fed.

In fact, the women kept their ears sharp so as to hear such remarks as, "Whoever made this custard pie knows how to bake pie!" The baker would never admit that she made it, but she would secretly vow that from now on, she would always take custard pie to any gatherings. They enjoyed making their families, friends, and neighbors happy.

So, as the women gathered to do their share, the men assembled to hear what *Shreiner* Dan (Carpenter Dan) had to say. Every carpenter crew needs a good foreman, and Dan was it.

"Now boys," he began. He called the men and everyone "boys." "We will need to work together if we want to get this barn up and ready to move into by tonight. I know we can do it. Let's divide up in groups of twelve and I'll assign you to your jobs. Then I'll tell all of you on my left here what I want you to do." So the work began as men tied their nail aprons and picked up hammers, ready for the task given them.

Sam Lapp strutted around as if he were head foreman. He noticed James Miller among a group of men getting ready to work on the south side. Just the sight of him riled Sam.

"Who asked him to come?" Sam muttered to himself. "Well, he had just better stay out of my way. Coming with his English clothes. He probably thinks he is some dude. Bet he can't even drive a nail straight."

What Sam didn't realize was that James was an excellent carpenter. His grandfather had been in that line of work and James seemed to have inherited it from him. This fact caught the eye of *Shreiner* Dan and he began to give James special tasks. Naturally, that didn't sit well with Sam, and he began to think of some way to make James look clumsy.

His chance came at lunchtime. Long tables had been made from boards laid across tressels and covered with newspapers. Close by, washtubs of water were placed under shade trees for the men to wash up. Becky was just setting a dish of hot noodles on the table as James walked toward one tub to wash up. They saw each other about the same time.

"Hello, Becky," James greeted her.

She smiled back as she said, "Well, hello. Guess you got your work cut out for you today."

"Guess so," he answered as he made his way on toward the line of men under the tree. Here was just the chance Sam Lapp had been waiting for. He stuck his foot out and tripped James, causing him to fall headfirst into the tub of water. Then Sam quickly turned and looked innocently the other way. But not quick enough, for Becky had seen what he had done.

"Well, James," laughed little Cristy Wengerd, "we know you are hungry, but take your time. We won't eat it all before you get there."

"I thought he was a Mennonite, but it looks to me like he is fixin' to be a Dunkard," Sam said, raising his voice extra loud for everyone to hear. The men laughed and some gave James a friendly slap on the back. James laughed with them while he dried his hair and face on the towel one of the men handed him.

"Guess I must be awful careless," he said. "It's good I had both feet on the ground and not on a scaffold twenty feet up." Becky thought he handled himself well. She was sure he knew who tripped him.

Looking in Becky's direction, Sam remarked again loudly, "I'd say if he didn't have his head in the clouds over a certain girl, he could see where he was going." James blushed slightly, but kept calm and shrugged it off.

The gall of that Sam Lapp! Becky could have made some statements, too, about being sly and unkind, but she was too much of a woman to retaliate.

Later in the afternoon, James took some more ribbing.

"Hey, James," Menno Swartz called to him during a lull in the noise of the hammers, "I've heard of falling for a girl, but never headlong into a tub of water." There was a lot of other joshing going on, too, so James didn't feel out of place.

The hammering, measuring, and sawing went on and soon the men were ready to put the framework in place. Everyone took his position. The women and children watched this awesome sight. Some men held the ropes, which had been fastened at various places. Others had long spiked poles to help push. Still others used their hands to lift and get it off the ground. But the grandest part of all was when *Shreiner* Dan would call out in his booming voice, "Heave-ho! Heave-ho!" And then, when every wall was set in place, a shout went up from men, women, and children alike. That is from all except some of the older sisters of the church. They thought it was much too noisy for meek and quiet Amish.

Now men swarmed all over the skeleton of the new barn. The rafters were put in place, the outside boards were nailed to the side framework, and the roof was begun. Those with no work to do on the outside began to put in horse stalls and stanchions for the cattle. The concrete floor had been poured before, so they could go right ahead.

"If I don't miss my guess," predicted Felty Mast, "Mony will have a new place for his cows tonight, come milking time."

"*Ya,*" answered Mose J., "if we stop talking and keep on working, I think he just might."

In the middle of the afternoon, the women sent some of the girls out to the barn with gallons of homemade lemonade. Each girl had a common cup to pass around, a thrifty practice supported by Jesus' example at the Last Supper. By now the men were thirsty. *Shreiner* Dan had put James in charge of the builders of the stalls for Mony's horses. Becky did not know this, but as she took a pitcher of the cold drink and entered the barn, she heard Sam Lapp say, "I hope you know what you're doing. My dad is particular about his horses. He likes for them to have plenty of room."

"Well, I'll try my best," James answered.

"Want some lemonade?" Becky asked, as she offered a tin cup of icy refreshment. Neither of the boys had heard her come inside.

"Why yes, I believe I will have some. It sure looks inviting," and James reached for the drink.

Like a flash, Sam's hand shot out and took the cup from Becky's hand.

"I'll drink first," he remarked. "You won't catch me drinking from the same cup a horse thief drinks from."

James's face colored. He had to bite his tongue so as not to retaliate. Becky stood there dumbfounded. They both knew what Sam was referring to. Whenever an Amishman thought someone was trying to win another person to their way of living, or to attend another church, they would call it horse-thieving.

Well, thought Becky, *I never even considered going out with Sam Lapp. He has no right to make it sound as if James were stealing me from him.*

As Sam was drinking the lemonade, James regained his composure, looked straight at Becky, and said, "Rebecca, our young folks are having a box social next Wednesday night. Would you like to come?"

"I sure would," she answered with a happy smile.

This was so unexpected to Sam. He began to sputter and choke on his mouthful of liquid. Spitting it out on the ground, he threw the cup down and walked away. James and Becky both laughed as James bent down to retrieve the empty, dented cup. He held it while she refilled it, and he drank gladly, regardless of who had sipped from it before.

Felty Mast's prediction had come true. By evening Emmanuel Lapp had a new barn. A salesman came by to try selling lightning rods to him, but Mony refused. "They are not for our people," he told the English man. "We trust God for our protection."

"That's good," said the salesman, "but look what happened to your old barn. Maybe God expects us to do what we can to keep these things from happening. I think you'd be wise to let me explain how it would help."

"My help comes from the Lord, and I expect he doesn't need mine." Mony told him. "Besides, look how our people stick together and work hard for each other when one of us has trouble. We don't need insurance and lightning rods and all that expensive stuff. We have the assurance of the love of our brothers in the church. And see what a nice big barn I have, much bigger and better than the other one. It keeps a community close when we bear each other's burdens."

What could anyone say to that? The man from town got in his car and left. He had not made a sale that day, but he had surely been given food for thought.

Evening came and with it milking time. All the utensils that had been taken to the Marner farm were carted back home. As Mr. Marner and Mony were loading the milk pails and ten-gallon cans on the hack (an open buggy with an extension box built on the back), Mony wanted to pay his friend for the use of his barn and feed. Mr. Marner would not hear of it.

"No, you are not paying one red cent. What are neighbors for if we can't help each other? Who knows, maybe tomorrow I'll need help. Then I won't feel so bad to call on you." He laughed at his last statement.

"You need never feel bad to ask me for help. And don't

you forget that." Emmanuel slapped the reins lightly on his horse's back and the hack, with its cargo, went rattling down the road.

On his way home, Mony Lapp thought much about how his church operated in just such times as he and his family experienced. Instead of holding insurance policies, each family of the church was assessed a certain amount, depending upon their financial status. This money was then collected as needed by the deacon of the church. Not only did members of one's own congregation give, but contributions came from many Amish churches, even in other states. If there were big hospital bills to be paid, a money shower was announced and printed in the weekly newspaper called *The Budget*. Mr. Lapp was confident that this was, by far, the better way.

Becky, too, had been deep in thought this evening. Why, oh why, had she told James Miller she would go to the box social with him? Was it to spite Sam? She didn't think so, although she still thought it funny that James asked her in Sam's presence. What would her parents say? And if this came before the church, what then? She knew the answers to both those questions fairly well, but didn't want to face up to them. If only her mother could see the difference between these two boys, she would understand. Becky was sure of it. Ellie Eash had hinted several times that perhaps her daughter didn't give Sam a chance and that maybe if she would try, she could find him nice after all.

That evening, during chore time, Sam offered to strain the milk from the overflowing pail Becky was about to empty. This wasn't like him at all, but soon she knew why he pretended to be so helpful.

Reaching for the pail and lifting it to the strainer, he said, "So, you are going with James Miller again. You do and I'll tell it to the preachers. Then you know what will happen. They will bring it to the whole church and you will have to make a public confession. You go and I'll tell."

Becky turned her nose up ever so slightly and said, "You tell and I'll go anyway!"

Rebecca surprised herself sometimes. But this was one time she didn't care if she *was* shocking. *Let Sam Lapp mind his own business,* she told herself.

7
A Box Social

As usual, David and Ellie Eash were glad to have their daughter home for the weekend. It was a time of catching up on all the current events for both parents and daughter.

"How does Mony like his new barn?" David asked. "Is it big enough for all his animals and hay?"

"He says it's a much nicer barn than he thought he would ever have. He can hardly believe the church would do all this for him."

"Well, I don't know why not. That is the way of our people," her father remarked.

"Dad, how come you always say 'our people'? A lot of men from other churches helped put up that barn, too," Becky reminded him.

"Well, yes, but our Amish people planned it."

"Do you think it's good for others who are not Amish to help us when we need help?"

"Sure, I guess so. Why? What makes you ask so many questions?"

"She has always been more curious than any of our others were, David," Ellie reminded him.

"Maybe that's why I'm the smartest," teased Becky. They all laughed at this statement. Becky had been trying to find a way to tell them she had promised James to go with him again, but the conversation was taking on a happy tone and she didn't want to spoil it.

Next morning she told her parents that if they were going into town she would like to go along. There were a few things she needed. David sometimes went alone, but today Ellie also needed some extra things, so both women decided to go.

"Ables' store is having a sale on jar lids and other canning things. I could use a large kettle as my big granite one is chipped so badly," remarked Ellie.

"You women are always looking for bargains. I wonder if you know one when you see one," David heckled.

Quick of wit and not to be outdone, his wife said, "Well, I got you, didn't I? And I don't think I made such a bad deal."

In continued good-natured conversation they started on their way to town. It was such a lovely day and, as the horse trotted briskly along, they enjoyed the countryside and one another's company. Their buggy was made to seat only two comfortably, so Becky sat on her mother's lap. She was a sprite of a girl, so Ellie didn't mind. As they passed by the Miller farm, they all waved to Mr. Miller and James, who were repairing fence close to the roadway.

"That Leroy Miller is sure a nice man," remarked David. "He would help anyone who is in need. A good worker, too, and so is that boy of his." This seemed to be the opportune time for Becky to make her move.

"Well, then, you shouldn't care if I go to a box social with James Miller this Wednesday night," she began. "He asked me and I think he is a nice fellow, too, same as you.

I said I'd go." There! She had done it. Becky felt her mother tense up even as she was speaking and she noticed David's mouth set firmly.

"Oh, Rebecca," her mother spoke first, "I thought you said you were only going with him once."

"I know and I really hadn't intended to, but Sam Lapp was so mean to James at the barn raising. When James asked me to go, I just said 'yes' without studying about it."

"What's to study?" David asked. "You know how Mom and I feel about it. This will cause trouble, not only with your family, but with the church also."

"But you just said James is a good worker and bragged about his dad. I think he must be very much like his father."

"Rebecca," said her dad, "it's one thing to be friendly and good neighbors to the Millers. It's another thing for you to *rumschpringe* (run around) with James. You are twenty-one and Mom and I can't make you do as we would like, but we hope you would want to." The rest of the way to town was traveled in strained silence or small talk.

Becky marched to the grocery store with an almost defiant air about her and made her purchase quickly. She did not want to use any of the Lapp's staples to prepare her food for Wednesday evening's social.

The thought of causing her parents unhappiness brought her some concern, but she had promised again and she would keep her word. Upon completing her mission at the grocery, she crossed the street to the five-and-dime store. She would need some crepe paper and ribbon to decorate her box. This taken care of, Becky made her way to the buggy, where she sat in deep thought waiting for her parents. Father had said that, while in town, Mother might as well stop by the eye doctor to have her glasses adjusted. This took a little extra time, so Rebecca tried to think of a way she could make her parents understand her feelings without hurting theirs. She dearly loved her mother and father. They had been so kind and loving to all of their children and to Grandma Maust and Esther, who lived in the *Dawdy Haus* (grandparents' small house).

David and Ellie appeared with arms loaded down with bags and packages.

"What did you do? Buy the whole town?" Becky asked jokingly. Usually such a remark would have produced jolly laughter and a suitable reply. But not this time. David and Ellie deposited their bundles in the back buggy box and solemnly climbed aboard. Becky dreaded the ride home. She did ask her mother if she had her glasses taken care of and was answered in the affirmative.

Wednesday afternoon, Becky approached Amanda Lapp with an unusual request. "Could I use the kitchen a little bit tonight after supper and this afternoon to bake a pie and fix some other things?"

"Well, I guess so," Amanda answered, rather taken aback. "Sure, go ahead if you want, but one pie isn't near enough for our family. I figured you knew that."

"No, it isn't for us here," Becky laughed. "It's for a young folk's get-together."

"That's funny," Mrs. Lapp said. "None of our boys said anything about going anywhere."

"Yes, I know," Becky informed her. "It isn't for the Amish *Yunga* (young folks). The Mennonite youth are having a box social and I'm invited."

She detected the coolness in Amanda Lapp's voice as she questioned, "Do your *Eldre* (parents) know about this?"

Becky assured her they did, but made a special attempt to make certain she told her that they did not approve.

"I should think not," remarked Mrs. Lapp.

Becky almost wished she hadn't told her employer why she needed the use of her kitchen. Before the afternoon was nearly over, Amanda had found countless extra things to be done, things that could have waited for another time. Fear began to creep into Becky's heart. What if James came for her and she didn't have her box of food prepared? Worse yet, what if she were not ready? Perhaps Amanda Lapp thought of what a good worker she had in Rebecca Eash. For, with just hardly enough time left, she released her *Maut* to get things together.

Rebecca quickly put her ingredients together for a shoofly pie and popped it into the oven. Then she fixed ham-and-cheese sandwiches, deviled eggs, and two small cups of potato salad. She ran upstairs and decorated a shoe box with pretty lavender crepe paper and yellow ribbon. She had purchased a big yellow bow for the top. This completed, she went back to the kitchen to check on her pie and clean up the dishes she had used.

Little Sara met her as she came through the door. "Umm," she said. "Somesing sure smells good. What are you making?"

"Shoofly pie," Becky told her.

"Goody. I like it real good."

Oh, thought Becky, *how can I tell her it's for me to take to the social?*

"I'll tell you a secret, Sara. The pie is not for here, but I will only need two pieces. So tomorrow, if it's all right with your mom, I will make some more. We will hide the pie I don't need tonight and then tomorrow we will eat it with the rest. Okay?"

Sara didn't understand and Rebecca didn't have time to explain. She didn't eat supper with the Lapp family that evening, which brought questions from the menfolk, but Amanda said she would talk about it later when the *Kinder* (children) were in bed.

Becky sat on the porch swing while the family ate their evening meal. She wished they would finish quickly. Many thoughts tumbled through her mind as she looked forward to seeing James again. Finally, the younger children came out to the porch. Rebecca went inside to help clear away the dishes. In her hurry she dropped a dinner plate. It shattered into many small pieces.

"*Schusslich* (careless haste) doesn't pay," remarked Sam with a sneer. "You going somewhere again?" Becky did not answer, but took the broom and dustpan and began to sweep up the broken pieces. "You'd better be glad that wasn't Mom's good set of dishes," Sam reminded her.

"I am," she answered curtly.

Becky apologized to Amanda and said she would try to replace the broken dish. But Mrs. Lapp said there was no need for that since her everyday dishes were just odds and ends.

When Rebecca came downstairs dressed up and ready to get her food put in her decorated box, she was glad that the men had gone back to the barn to curry the horses. The younger Lapp children stared in amazement at the lovely box she carried.

"Why are you putting food in it?" Sara asked. So Rebecca explained to her what a box social was.

"I hope I can go to a box social when I'm big," little Katie Lapp exclaimed.

"Katie," Amanda reprimanded her daughter, "you don't even think such things."

Neither Katie nor Sara knew why you didn't think about it. Everything looked so pretty, but they said no more. All they could do was stare in openmouthed wonder. Their wonder and amazement grew even more as James Miller drove in and escorted Becky, box and all, out to his shiny car and drove down the lane and out of sight.

"I've never been to a box social before," Becky confided in James. "I'm not sure what to do."

"You have nothing to worry about. Us fellows are the ones with a problem."

"Why?" asked Becky.

"Your part was finished when you had the food and box all made up. But now all the boxes are put together and will be auctioned off to the highest bidder. Whoever buys your box will also share the food with you. In other words, you will eat together. If I want to buy your box, and I do, and someone else outbids me, then I'm in trouble. See what I mean?" James asked.

"I hope you buy mine," Becky replied. After she said it, she felt very forward.

Quite a few other young people were already there when they arrived. Becky and Susan saw each other about the same time and paired up right away. Several other girls joined them.

"Becky," said Susan, "how long will you be working for Mony Lapp's?"

"Oh, I don't really know," Rebecca answered. "I haven't set any special time."

"Good," Susan said, "then you haven't promised anything. I know about a family in town, friends of the people I work for. They are looking for a hired girl. He is a doctor and I know they pay extra good wages. It would not be near as much work either or as hard as where you are now. From what you told me, you would like another place. Are you interested?"

"It sounds really good, but how would I get there?"

"Oh, they would come and get you Monday morning.

and bring you home Friday afternoon," answered Susan.

"Oh, that would be nice," Becky exclaimed. "Just think, I'd have more time to do my own things."

"The boys are ready to start the auction," said Mr. King, the owner of the home where the group had gathered.

The boxes, which had been so beautifully decorated, were all brought concealed in ordinary brown paper bags. This was done so none of the boys knew whose box they were buying. Mrs. King had received them as they arrived, took them to another room where she removed them from the bags, and arranged them on a table. What a pretty sight they were in their colorful array. Freddie Ropp was the auctioneer and he was a good one. The money taken in that evening was to go for missions, so it was the desire of everyone that a good amount was raised.

How James wished he knew which box Becky brought. He looked them over carefully and finally decided to bid on a pink one with a frilly white bow. It cost him a pretty penny and brought gales of laughter when his sister, Susan, went and stood by his side, indicating he had just purchased her lunch.

"Are you too bashful to eat with me?" Susan asked impishly.

"Not at all," her brother answered, "but I hope you know I'm a big eater."

"I sure ought to. I've watched you often enough," teased Susan.

John Summer bought Rebecca's box. She shyly walked to his side, but soon found him to be very friendly as they chatted and then ate together.

The evening was spent in some Bible study and singing. Several games were played outdoors and soon it was time to go home. Henry Kaufman, the treasurer of the group, reported they had taken in two hundred and forty-three dollars, for which they were grateful.

"Did you enjoy the evening?" James asked as they started on the way to Lapp's place.

"Yes, I did, and I'm learning things about the Bible I didn't know before. Guess it's because I don't understand German too well," Becky answered.

"Well, I'd be glad to have you come often, if you'd like," James informed her.

"I'd like to, but I will think about it."

Rebecca didn't want this night to end.

8
Amish Standards

Rebecca sensed something was amiss the next morning as soon as she came downstairs to begin her day's work. Mrs. Lapp, who was generally cheerful and greeted her with a smile, barely looked at her and never even answered the *Maut's* good morning.

"What's on the list for today's work?" Becky asked.

"Same as always," was the only response she got. She didn't try to pursue the conversation further, but made her way to the milk house. There she put the empty pails and cans onto the cart and headed for the barn. The cows were already in their places, eating grain eagerly, and switching contentedly.

"So! You are late in coming out for milking this morning," Sam heckled. "Better learn to stay home weeknights. Then you can get up on time in the mornings. What are my folks paying you for, anyway?"

Becky knew she was ready to start the milking at her usual time, but she wasn't even giving Sam the satisfaction of an argument. Taking a pail she sat on the little three-legged stool and started to milk. She could hear Sam still mumbling something but couldn't understand what he was saying.

At the breakfast table a bit later, she could tell there was a strange coolness toward her which she had never experienced to such an extent before. While they were eating, Franie Marner came by to see if she might borrow some flour. Her husband had neglected to buy any the last time she had sent for some at the General Store.

"That man," she began. "I always say 'if his head weren't fastened, he would forget that too.'" Normally, this would have produced a round of laughter from the Lapp clan. Mrs. Marner wondered about this when her remark hardly brought forth a chuckle.

"Oh, by the way," she said, "Did you hear that Johnnie Dans have a baby girl?"

"No, I hadn't heard," Amanda Lapp answered.

"She was born last evening around six and they named her Mary Lou," Franie informed them.

"Oh my! I don't like to hear that," Amanda exclaimed.

"What!" ejaculated Mrs. Marner. "You mean you don't like to hear about it when someone has a new baby?"

"No, I didn't mean it that way. I mean, I don't like to hear when they name them so fancy. It isn't for our people and, besides, I've heard when a person has a middle name it means they will experience a hard death."

There was that expression again. Becky had heard it so often from her father. "Our people." *Why are we any different from any other people? And how did anyone know why some have a calmer, easier passing from this life than others? Besides, what did one's name have to do with it?* Mrs. Marner also seemed amazed at such a belief.

"I've never heard the like of any such notion before. But I suppose everybody has their peculiarities."

"Well," answered Amanda, "now I didn't say I believe that. I only said I've heard some think that way. But I don't care for fancy names. Plain and simple, that should be good enough for anyone. Especially for us Amish."

Mrs. Marner thanked her for the flour and, promising to return it after her next trip to town, she made her way down the road toward home.

So that's it, thought Rebecca. *Because we are Amish, we can't have what other people have, even if they are not wicked themselves. Now I know why they say "our people." They mean Amish.*

Breakfast over with, Amanda told Becky to follow her to the garden while Sara and Katie did up the dishes. They had just stepped inside the gate when Mrs. Lapp said, "Becky, I must tell you something. I'm sorry and I hardly know how to begin, but Mony says I have to." She paused as if she did not know how to approach the subject. Her hired girl decided she would come to her aid.

Being reasonably sure what was coming, Rebecca asked, "Is it about my going with the young folks from the other church?"

"Yes," answered Amanda, relieved that she need not bring up the matter. "I'm really sorry to say this but Mony says I have to let you go. You have been such a good *Maut* and I'll sure miss you. I don't know how I'll get the work done. But I guess there will be a way."

Rebecca's heart went out in sympathy to Amanda Lapp. She had such a large family, but maybe she could find another girl to help her.

"I'm sorry too, in a way," Rebecca said. "You are a good person to work for, but maybe it's for the best that I leave."

"How do your parents feel about your *Rumschpringe* (running around) with boys and girls from the other group?" Amanda inquired of her.

"They don't like it either, but I think those boys and girls are just as nice as many other *Yunga*."

"I didn't say they weren't," Amanda ventured, "but they do drive cars and have telephones, electric, and have church houses, which we, as Amish, don't allow."

"I know," Becky answered, "and I don't mean to cause trouble. It's just that I enjoy their company and know they are Christians."

"Well, you just be careful you don't get in too deep," admonished her employer. "I hear they take their Bibles along to most of their meetings. There could be a danger of adding to or taking away from the Scriptures."

Rebecca was shocked by this kind of reasoning, but only asked, "How long do you want me yet?"

"You can stay until the end of the week," she was told. That would mean only two more days, since this was Thursday. She heard Sam's voice coming across the outer yard and, all of a sudden, she felt happier than she had in a long time. It would be a relief not to have him heckle her. Yet she did not want to have any ill feelings toward anyone.

Rebecca thought the time she had left to work at the Emmanuel Lapp home was the longest two days she had ever spent in her entire life.

Little Sara and Katie Lapp were sad when Saturday evening came and their *Maut* told them she would not be back on Monday morning.

"But who will work for us?" asked Katie.

"I don't know, but your mother will find someone. I'm sure of that."

"We don't want someone, we just want you," Sara told her, as two big tears ran down her cheeks and splashed on her apron.

"Now don't you two make it so hard for me to leave," Rebecca said lovingly. "I'll see you at church and maybe sometimes you can come and sit with me during preaching."

This brought some comfort to her little friends. But on later Sundays they were never allowed to sit by her, and Rebecca knew why.

When she arrived home that evening, her mother wondered why she brought her two large suitcases and several boxes of things. This was so different from her usual arrival. Most of her Sunday clothes were left at the Eash's house and her everyday work clothes she kept at her place of employment. She only had to carry her personal belongings back and forth. Toothpaste and toothbrush, hairbrush and comb, her purse, and a few other items didn't take long to pack. Roy Lapp had brought her home. She was glad it hadn't been Sam. At least the ride was much more pleasant in Roy's company. He helped her with her suitcases and other things.

After his departure, Ellie asked her daughter, "Rebecca, are you coming home to stay?"

There was no getting around it. Her mother would have to hear the truth. "Yes, Mom, I guess I am. The Lapps told me on Thursday."

"But why?" asked Ellie. "I'm sure Amanda needs help with her large family."

"Guess I may as well tell you," Becky told her. "It's just because I went with James Miller to that box social."

"I knew that would cause trouble, Rebecca. Deacon Byler was here to see you this week, but you weren't home, of course. He said he would stop by another time. Oh, Becky, why can't you be satisfied to go with our *Yunga*?" Ellie asked with a sigh.

"I like our young people a lot, but James and Susan are good friends, too. I enjoy being with them and I don't see what is wrong about that."

"Rebecca, do you remember my school girlfriend,

67

Missy, that I told you about? We were such good friends and I always wished I could have things that she had. But do you remember how I told you she came to visit one day and how she had changed so? It made me ever so sad and yet, how thankful I was that our friendship terminated before my *Rumschpringe* years. Now, I know not all English people turn out like she did; probably most are fine Christians, or at least good moral folk. Yet why take a chance with those not brought up according to the *alt Ordnung* (old standards). Please think carefully, Rebecca. Your father and I want only the best for you." What a long speech for Ellie Eash, but she felt she must do all she could to admonish her lovely young daughter.

Becky just nodded, then took her suitcases upstairs and began to unpack.

Mr. Eash had been down in the orchard checking the fruit trees and inspecting his beehives when his daughter came home. Upon entering the living room, he heard footsteps upstairs. "Is Becky home?" he asked his wife.

"Yes, she is, David. She came home about thirty minutes ago. Roy brought her." Ellie's voice trembled a bit as she spoke.

"What's wrong Mom?" David asked, "Don't you feel well?"

"*Ach*, yes, I feel all right. It's Becky. She got fired at the Lapps. They don't want her to come because she went with James Miller again."

"I'll just need to have a talk with her, Ellie," David told her. "She is a sensible girl and I think she will listen."

"I know, David," Ellie said, "but she is twenty-one and her own boss, so we can't make her do as we say."

"That's true," David Eash agreed, "but she knows the rules of the church and we brought her up in the ways of the Amish."

"Let's not worry about it. We will talk to her and we will pray."

Rebecca did not return downstairs as soon as she had put things in place. Taking her Bible she sat on the edge of her bed and turned to the fifth chapter of Matthew. She read the first sixteen verses. Then she knelt by her bed and prayed silently, but fervently. Refreshed from her communion with God, she joined her parents downstairs.

"Hello, Rebecca," David greeted his daughter.

"Hi, Dad," she answered. "What did you do today to stay out of mischief?"

David didn't answer immediately, and when Rebecca looked at him, she knew it wasn't the right time for bantering.

"I was busy enough," he answered curtly.

It was warm in the house so Becky decided to sit on the swing awhile. Her Aunt Esther, who still lived in the *Dawdy Haus*, saw her there and decided to join her.

"Hello, Rebecca," she called as she came across the lawn. "Want someone to talk to?"

"Sure," answered Becky. "Come and visit awhile." Esther didn't know how happy Rebecca was for her company.

"Well, what's new?" asked Esther.

"There's something strange I've never heard before. Mrs. Marner came to borrow some flour from Amanda Lapp and she told her Johnnie Dans have a baby girl."

"That's strange?" interrupted Esther laughingly. "What's strange about having a baby girl?"

"No, silly," said Becky giggling, "wait until you hear the rest of it."

By this time, David and Ellie had heard the laughing and came out on the porch to see who Becky was talking to.

"Sit down," invited Esther, "and listen to what Becky is telling me."

They found seats and Becky related the incident to them.

"What do you think about giving babies two names?" asked Becky.

"I never gave it a thought," Ellie said. "But I don't see how that could have anything to do with a person's death."

"Neither do I," Esther agreed. "But, then, I guess we all have our own peculiar beliefs. I know I always think I can tell when it's going to rain because Teddy eats grass." Teddy was her little terrier.

They were still sitting on the porch talking when they saw a buggy come down the road and slow by their drive.

"Looks like Amos Byler," David said.

Amos Byler was the deacon in their church. When a member disobeyed or failed to conform to the rules of the church, it was his responsibility to approach them. Rebecca was sure she knew why he was coming.

"Wonder what brings him here?" Esther remarked. She had not known about Rebecca Eash going out with James Miller, the Mennonite young man.

"He wants to speak with Rebecca, I suppose," David answered for Esther's sake.

Amos pulled up to the front gate and stopped.

"Wie geht's? (how do you do)?" he said to no one in particular and yet to all of them.

David returned the greeting. They spoke briefly and then David invited him to come in.

"No," he said, "I want to talk to Rebecca alone. Would you come out here?"

Obediently, Rebecca got up and went out to the buggy. Amos remained seated and David, Ellie, and Esther went inside to their own houses and with their own thoughts.

9
Worldly Temptations

The Monday after Deacon Byler had come to talk with Rebecca Eash, her father, David, approached her about the same matter. Becky had just finished helping her mother with the breakfast dishes and was going out to weed some flower beds.

"Becky," David stopped her, "let's sit here on the swing. I need to talk with you."

Instinctively she knew the reason, but she asked anyway. "What do you want to talk about?"

"I think you know, Rebecca. Don't you think it would be better for all concerned if you didn't go out with James Miller any more?"

"What do you have against James or any of the Millers?" his daughter asked.

"Nothing. They are nice people. It's just that their ways are more modern than ours. Many things they have are *verbodde* (forbidden) in our church. You see, if you start out giving in to a few things, soon you will want more and more. Finally, there is a danger of saying nothing matters and you can have or do as you please. Some say that already and add 'as long as the heart is right.' But if the heart is right, we don't seek after things; we seek to please God."

"Can't we please God and still enjoy some things that are more convenient, as long as we don't put them first in our lives?" asked Becky.

"*Ach*, Rebecca, you make it so hard for me to explain with all your questions. Can't you just be satisfied with the way we live? Especially if what you do will cause problems in the church and maybe even in your own family?"

"I don't mean to cause any problems, but it's just that I find their Bible study so interesting and the young people are fun to be with."

"That's another thing," remarked Mr. Eash. "We must be careful we don't add or detract from the Word of God. They might do this by discussing the Scriptures."

"But how else will we learn if we don't talk about the Bible teaching?" she wondered.

"We will just listen to the preachers in our church. They can tell us all we need to know and we can read it for ourselves," David told her.

"I do read the Bible, but, Dad, I often wonder what so many things mean. I'm thankful for the many times you and Mom showed me right from wrong, and there is so much I want to learn." Becky spoke in all sincerity from her heart.

"Well," her father said, "your mother and I have both talked with you and I'm sure you know our desire for you. Sure there are some Christians besides our own Amish people." As an afterthought, David remarked, "I'm afraid not all our people are Christian, sad to say. It's just that I think our way of life is a more simple, contented, quiet way and there are, perhaps, less temptations than some other beliefs. We can't force you to do as we wish, but I would advise you to hold fast to what you have been taught. It's time to get to work, Becky." With that, he got up and made his way off the porch and across the yard toward the barn.

Rebecca watched him go and a bit of her heart went with him. She dearly loved her parents and in no way did she wish to hurt them. Why did life have to be so complicated?

She went out to where Ellie was working in the flower beds and began to weed. But all the while she worked and even in small conversation with her mother, Becky's thoughts rambled. Like the tall flowers nodding in the wind, she felt like she was being tossed about. The deacon had told her that though he didn't want to do it, if she continued riding in a car for pleasure, he would have to demand a confession before the church. *It isn't just for pleasure,* she reasoned; *it's also to be with others my age interested in learning more about God's Word.* Yet she had to admit she liked the company of Susan and James.

What was she going to do about a job? She couldn't just stay at home. Every good Amish girl earns her bread and butter. She had heard Mike's Levi and his wife were needing help for a few months anyway. Maybe she would ask Dad for the rig to drive over after supper and see if they had found someone yet.

"I've been bending over so long that my back hurts so, and I don't know if I'll ever be able to straighten up," Ellie told her daughter.

"Well, Mom, you needn't stay out here any longer," Becky said. "You go on in and rest while I finish this."

Grateful for the offer, Ellie went to the pump for a cool drink of water and then sat in the shade for a short rest. Rebecca was so busy and deep in thought that she didn't hear her Aunt Esther until she stood right by her and spoke.

73

"Would you like some help?" she asked.

"Oh, Esther, I didn't hear you coming. Yeah, a little help would be nice. Mom worked out here too long, I'm afraid. She said she didn't know if she could ever straighten up again. Her back hurt so," Becky said.

"Well, I could have come out earlier if I would have known what you were doing," Esther answered.

"Have you been busy with the store?" Becky inquired.

"Just by spells. You know how it goes. Seems like for a while nobody comes and then they all need something at once."

They worked on and before long had finished the task of weeding.

"I've made a pitcher of lemonade," Esther said. "Why don't you come in and we will have a glass full to cool us off."

"Sounds good to me," answered Becky, accepting the offer. Somehow she sensed that her aunt wanted to talk some more.

They washed up at the sink in the kitchen with cool water from the little hand pump. Esther poured two refreshing glasses of lemonade and they sat at the kitchen table to enjoy their drink.

"So," Esther began, "are you through working for Mony's?"

"Yes, I guess I am," confessed Becky.

"That's a surprise to me," her aunt stated. "With such a large family as they have, I assumed Amanda would need you for a long time."

"Maybe this is as good a time as any to tell you why I'm not going to be working there any more," offered Rebecca. "It's because I've been going with James Miller and Susan to some of their Mennonite youth meetings. Mrs. Lapp said Mony told her she can't keep me any longer." If Rebecca Eash expected an outburst of disapproval from her aunt, she didn't get one.

Instead, Esther calmly and quietly answered, "I've heard some talk to that effect. Have your parents said much about it?"

"They have both talked to me and let me know they are not happy with the situation. Oh, Esther, I don't want to make trouble, but I think James and his family are so nice. Why is it wrong to be friends with them?"

"I like the Millers too," Esther told her. "And I have many non-Amish friends. It isn't that we don't approve of people; it's the things they allow that are forbidden for us. Things that are worldly," she added.

"But why are cars and electricity worldly, Esther?" questioned Becky.

"Of themselves, they may not be," Esther answered, "but look what many people do with cars. They drive so fast, no longer content to take time to meditate, to visit with their neighbors, and to enjoy the things around them. They can go places where you can't go with a horse and buggy. It just seems there are so many more temptations with modern things. People who have electricity now have radios and I've even heard of some who have a box in their home; they call it TV. Many pictures come on this box and most are not good, from what I hear tell."

"I never saw such a box at the Millers' home and we didn't go any place except to the young folks' literary. Oh, we did stop in town one Wednesday evening for some ice cream. Couldn't you go to places you shouldn't with a horse and buggy, too?" Becky asked.

"Sure you could," Esther agreed, "but you are not apt to drive a rig into the city, now are you?" Both laughed at the thought.

"I'd better be getting over into the house or Mom will wonder what happened to me," said Becky.

"Wait a minute. I have something to tell you before you

75

leave," Esther informed her niece. "I'm getting married this next winter, but don't you tell."

"What!" exclaimed Becky. She felt as if she could have been knocked over with a feather. She had imagined her aunt would stay single. The *Dawdy Haus* wouldn't be the same without her. What about the store? Who would take care of that? Becky just always thought Esther would be there. Always!

"Well, don't look so shocked Becky," Esther admonished. "You seem speechless. Am I so old I can't marry?"

"Oh, no—no. I guess I'm just so surprised. I didn't even know you were seeing anyone. Is it someone I know, or aren't you telling yet?"

"He is not from around here. I met him a little over a year ago when some of us 'old maids' went to Florida for a few weeks. He is from Iowa. We have been writing regularly and he has come to see me several times."

"You sure kept it a secret. Do my folks know it yet?" Rebecca asked.

"I told your mom and I suppose she told your dad, as he has made several little teasing remarks."

"That's Dad all right," answered Becky. "If he has teased you, he must know."

"Well, the reason I told you is because I'm going to be doing some canning and making other changes that I knew you would wonder about. I'll need to get rid of the store, too. That's one thing I know I'll miss. But, if I have to choose between a husband and a store, I'll pick the man. I can have a store anytime I please, but a husband only when he pleases."

They both laughed again.

"I'm happy for you," Becky told her aunt. "Will you live around here? I hope so," she quickly added.

"Probably not," Esther answered. "I imagine we will live in Iowa on his farm."

That made Becky rather sad. Esther had always been her favorite. On her way back to her own house, Becky thought, *How full of changes life is.*

She opened the screen door and went to the kitchen to help her mother prepare the noon meal. She must think of a new place to work. Once more she thought of Mike's Levi and his family. *That would be my best bet,* she decided. *I'm glad that's settled.*

10
A Wild Ride

"Dad," Becky approached her father at the dinner table. "Dad, may I have the rig tonight to drive over to Mike's Levi's place? I need to see about work and I heard she needs a *Maut.*"

"Well," answered David, "Patsy has thrown a shoe, but if you think you can handle Babe, you may take her."

"But David," Ellie protested, "you know how spirited Babe is. She shies so easily at cars and trucks. And look how she runs so fast. Do you think it would be safe?"

"I would go the back road, Mom. There is not much chance of meeting a car on that cow path," laughed Becky.

"I think she will be safe enough," David said.

"I'll be real careful," promised Becky, noticing her mother's worried expression.

The afternoon was spent washing windows, cleaning screens, and scrubbing the porch floor. Mrs. Eash, like most Amish, kept an immaculate house. Some even claimed her floor was clean enough to use for a table.

Ellie knew this was not so, but she wanted to live according to Proverbs thirty-one, which describes a virtuous woman. And to her family, she *was* more precious than jewels.

After supper David Eash hitched his spirited horse to the buggy for Becky. With a wave of his hand and another warning to be careful, he watched his daughter drive out of sight. Babe was already running at a full trot, but David had confidence that all would be well.

Rebecca was enjoying the fast ride, the wind blowing in her face, and the excitement of it all. Very soon she would reach her destination. Then she saw it. A car was approaching rapidly. Dust was flying as it came tearing down the narrow, gravel road. Rebecca could see the car was full of young folks, screaming, laughing, and waving. Babe shied and began to jump.

When Becky tightened her hold on the reins, Babe reared. Then she began to run faster than she had ever run before. There was no controlling her. The car had turned around and was coming from behind, blowing its horn. This only made matters worse. The car careened past, scraping the buggy wheels as it went.

Becky caught sight of a young Mennonite boy (the owner of the car) who had a reputation of being "wild," as the Amish call it. She also saw Sam Lapp leering and grinning at her.

That's the last she knew, until she opened her eyes in the hospital. Everything looked so fuzzy and strange. She kept seeing her mother and father close to her, then they weren't there at all. Her eyes didn't want to remain open, and oh, how her head hurt! Someone kept calling her name.

I must get up, she thought. *I must go help with the chores.* But her legs wouldn't move. They were too heavy. She tried and tried. Now she heard an unfamiliar voice. It seemed to say, "Just relax. Relax. Relax." She felt a little sting, and then came blissful sleep.

"Mother," David Eash told his wife, "You have to go home and get some rest. It's been four days now. Esther said she will stay here and we will come in the morning. I promise you we will be here early. Mr. Marner and Mr. Miller both offered to bring us anytime."

But no amount of pleading could persuade Ellie to leave her unconscious daughter.

"Just bring me a clean change of clothes," she answered. "I've been given permission to wash up right here in this bathroom. I can't leave, David, I just can't. Please don't make me," she begged.

"All right, Mom," David said, much to Ellie's relief. "I'll have to go home and look after things, but I promise to be back in the morning. If you need me before then, call the Millers. They said no matter what time of the night, they will be available." His voice almost broke as he said his good-bye. "I'll pray," he told his wife and then left the room quietly.

Mr. Marner was waiting in the lobby, but when he saw David coming down the hall, he rose to meet him. He asked that now-familiar question, "Any change?"

"Well, it seemed like she was trying to open her eyes and she stirred more, but I don't believe she knew what was going on. The nurse came and gave her a shot and she just lay there, same as before," he said dejectedly.

"Wonder why they keep giving her shots whenever she seems to respond a little," Mr. Marner remarked.

"The doctor told us they don't want her to come out of this too quickly or it could throw her into shock," David told him.

"Yes, I've heard of that before. At least it's encouraging that she shows signs of regaining consciousness," his friend stated.

"I will ask our neighbor, Mr. Miller, to bring me over in the morning," David told his driver. "You have made so many trips and it's so far from your place to pick me up here."

"Oh, I don't mind, but it's up to you," Mr. Marner said.

"Why don't we do that then and maybe later I'll call on you again." So it was decided.

During the night, Becky opened her eyes and it sounded as though she was trying to talk, then she slipped back into oblivion again. However, Ellie was so glad she stayed, for in the early morning hours, Becky did speak. Something about a green olive tree.

"Becky," said her mother softly, "It's me. I'm here. What is it you are saying? What do you want?"

Her daughter did not answer right away. So, thinking perhaps if she spoke to her in the German dialect, she said, "Becky, *was wit du* (what do you want)?"

It seemed to strike a familiar chord, for Rebecca said, "Mom, why are you so far away?"

"I'm not, Rebecca. I'm right here. See, I'm holding your hand. Can't you feel my hand?"

"I don't want you to be sad. I don't mean to be a bad girl. . . . " Her voice tapered off to a mere whisper.

"You are not, Becky. You are not a bad girl," her mother assured her, but Becky seemed to have drifted from her again.

If only David were here. Ellie knew he would come as soon as possible.

Mr. Miller had an appointment in another town around nine, so he asked David if his son, James, could take him to the hospital.

"Sure," David said, "that won't be any problem as long as it doesn't put you out any."

"Not at all. And anytime we can be of help, just let us know."

So that is how it came about that David was sitting beside the very young man who was keeping company with his daughter without his approval. *At a time of crisis you don't think about such things as different beliefs,* reasoned David. Had James Miller known what his Amish neighbor was thinking, he couldn't have agreed more.

"I'll just drop you off and come back this evening, if that's all right," James told David.

"Yes, that's what I figured," David agreed. "You can come around five, if it's okay with you."

"That would be fine. I'll see you then," James answered. "Or, if you would like, I can do your chores and pick you up after evening visiting hours," he offered as an afterthought.

"That would be awful nice of you, but I hate to ask."

"You didn't; I just offered. After all, what are neighbors for? I think I still know how to milk a cow," James laughed.

"I'm sure you do," answered David. "We just have the one cow to milk. My wife's sister lives in the small house. She can tell you where things are and take care of the milk."

Ellie was pleased that David was going to stay all day. She told him how their daughter had responded early in the morning, but they both wondered at what she said.

"She is just *verhuddelt noch* (mixed up yet)," David comforted Ellie.

"Maybe it's the medicine she is getting in all those shots," answered Mrs. Eash.

Around three o'clock in the afternoon, Rebecca opened her eyes again. Looking around the room, she asked, "*Wo bin ich* (where am I)?"

"You are at the Lanyale Hospital, Becky," her father answered.

"Why, how did I get here?" she wanted to know.

"Don't you remember at all?" inquired Ellie.

"No, Mom, I don't. What's wrong with my legs? They feel so heavy, and my head hurts."

"Well, Rebecca, you were in an accident, but you will be all right; I am sure of that. You took Babe to go over to Mike's Levis' to look for a job. Something happened that must have scared Babe and you had a buggy wreck."

"How bad am I hurt? Can't I walk? How long have I been here? What day is this?" Becky asked one question after another.

"Whoa now," David said, "don't go so fast! One thing at a time. Both of your legs are broken, but the doctor says you are young and your bones will mend and you will walk again. It will take time, sure, but we have more time than money, I always say." His joke fell a little flat. "Your one wrist is fractured and you do have a head injury. That is why your head hurts so. But we are so *dankbaar* (thankful) that you are still with us." David had to fight back the tears, tears of joy and relief that his daughter was awake and talking.

"You had better rest now, Becky," her mother advised her.

"Don't cry, Mom," Becky said. Ellie could not hide her tears as her husband did. She let them flow freely and felt relief.

"May we come in?"

David and Ellie both turned toward the door. They hadn't heard anyone coming down the hall.

"Oh, yes, come right in," Ellie said. "Look, Becky, Susan and James are here."

Rebecca turned her head slightly and tried to smile. She looked so pale and her head was wrapped almost entirely in bandages.

"How are you feeling, Becky?" asked her friend Susan.

"Little bit better," came the weak reply.

"We won't stay," James informed her. "Just thought we would stop in for a short prayer and to say hello."

Becky smiled faintly.

"Do you mind if we have a prayer? Then we'll wait for you in the lounge," James addressed David.

"Well, yes, I suppose that would be all right," answered Mr. Eash. He was accustomed to silent prayer or else reading from a prayer book. But he could not object to the few sincere words James prayed.

"We will be back when you feel better," Susan told Becky. Then turning to David, she said, "You and your wife just stay as long as you want to. We don't mind waiting." With that remark, she waved to her friend and left the room with her brother.

Rebecca heard her parents talking and she was glad to hear her dad say, "Those are two of the nicest young folks I've ever met."

Her mother agreed. "If only they were Amish though," said Ellie.

"Well," answered David, "maybe it doesn't matter so much what name they go by as how they live."

Had Becky heard right? She wondered if she was still in a coma or dreaming. It all seemed so unreal. She did not want to hear different from what she thought she heard, so she said nothing.

In her days of convalescence, Rebecca Eash had many visitors, Amish, Mennonite, and English friends and neighbors. Most of those visiting were younger people her own age. Generally she enjoyed the callers. But one came whom she could not enjoy: Sam Lapp. He made a remark that perhaps the Lord was trying to teach her something for going out with young people other than her own kind.

"And what is my kind?" she asked.

"Evidently not one who knows how to handle a horse or you could have controlled her before the car turned around and caught up with you again."

David, who was in the room with Becky at the time, looked sharply at Sam.

"How do you know that, Sam?" he asked.

Too late Sam realized his mistake. Grabbing his hat from the chair he had placed it on, he left very quickly.

Now it began to come back to Becky. Slowly she saw the car filled with young rowdies, waving and yelling. Yes, now she began to remember.

11
Taffy Pull and Singing

It took many long weeks before Rebecca was able to come back home. True to the doctor's predictions, her bones mended nicely. She was able to walk with crutches by late fall. Her parents gave her the best of care and tried to find ways to help pass the time. They decided to invite all the Amish young people from the three district churches on a Friday evening for a singing and a taffy pull.

Becky was delighted.

"Oh, Mom, may I invite James and Susan too?" she asked, "I have gone with them several times. Maybe they would enjoy coming to some of our get-togethers."

"I'll have to ask your father," answered Ellie. "But I don't see what harm it could do."

Later that evening, Becky said, "Have you asked Dad yet?"

"Asked him what?" Ellie acted so innocent. She knew very well what her daughter meant. But she still liked to play little tricks.

"You know, Mom. If we can invite the Miller boy and girl."

"Oh, you mean Susan," and Ellie paused on purpose.

"Yes, I mean Susan and James," Becky replied exasperatedly.

"Guess I may as well ask him if I want any rest," Ellie remarked with a smile. "Are you sure they want to come?" she asked.

"I think they would like it. Only one way to find out though."

"Okay, Becky, I'll ask David tonight at suppertime. By the way, what do you want to eat tonight? Sometimes I run out of ideas," Ellie admitted.

"Let's have *kalte Brockelsupp* (cold milk soup). I'm hungry for that and lettuce sandwiches," her daughter replied. Cold milk soup was a regular summer evening meal at their home.

"What fruit do you want in the soup?" Ellie asked. Since it was late in the fall, much of the summer fruit was no longer available. It had been canned for the winter months to come.

"Do we have any bananas? I like banana soup real good."

"Yes, I bought some in town last week. If the price goes up any more, we won't be buying very many. I'm glad our late lettuce did so well. That's what we will have then. Cold banana soup and sandwiches," Mrs. Eash decided.

Becky could taste it now; the homemade bread and butter with crisp leaves of lettuce sandwiched in-between and a soup plate filled with cold creamy milk, sweetened with sugar, and the pieces of homemade bread and bananas floating in it. Her very favorite, though, was fresh strawberries in cold milk soup.

"David," Ellie began, after they were seated at the table, "Becky thinks it would be nice if we would invite James and Susan Miller for Friday night singing and taffy pull. What do you think?"

Becky held her breath as she waited anxiously for her father to answer.

"Well now," he spoke slowly, "seeing as how they were so helpful while our girl was in the hospital, I guess it would be the neighborly thing to do. It's all right by me. They might find us Amish are not so different from other folks after all." He laughed at this statement.

Becky sighed in relief. She would ask Esther to stop by on her way to the quilting at her friend Alta Yutzy's place and invite the Miller youths.

She could hardly wait for Friday to come. All morning she was doing little things around the house to help get things ready.

"Rebecca," said her mother, "after lunch you had better lay down for a while. I'm afraid you have been on your feet too much."

"*Ich kann net schlofe* (I can not sleep)," Becky replied.

"But you can at least rest. I noticed you are limping more again," Ellie remarked.

"All right, Mom, but I'm so excited I can hardly sit still."

"So I noticed. As soon as you get those potatoes peeled, everything will be ready to put on the stove, so it won't be long until lunch is ready."

Becky did lie down after lunch. But as she had predicted, she couldn't lie still, let alone sleep. Why was she so anxious? She thought about this. *It's because some of my Amish girlfriends are coming,* she told herself. But she knew that wasn't entirely true. She liked many of them, but they had never caused so much excitement before. They came faithfully to visit when she was bedfast. *It's Susan,* she decided. *That's why I'm so happy. Susan is a lot of fun and she helps me with things I don't understand. I'm sure it's Susan.* Then she took a really honest look at the situation and herself.

"No," she said out loud, "It's James." *Why do I like him better than any of the others?* It was a disturbing thought.

After an early supper, she helped Ellie boil the taffy so it would be just right for pulling when the young people arrived. It worked out perfectly. Ellie had begun pouring it into the buttered pans and Becky had begun spreading wax paper when they saw buggies, bicycles, and even walkers coming down the drive.

"They're here, Mom. Here they come," bubbled Rebecca.

"Calm down once, Becky," Ellie told her daughter. "Set some butter out so we have plenty for greasing hands. You can't handle taffy with dry hands you know."

"Yeah, I know," Becky replied, setting several dishes on the large table.

After everyone was ready, they paired off by numbering. There were a few more boys than girls. Sam Lapp and his rowdy group were there. Sam happened to be the partner of a cousin of Becky. Becky felt sorry for her cousin Katie, but she was also glad he wasn't with her. She was paired with a good Amish friend, but time and again she caught herself only half-listening to his conversation. Her gaze kept wandering to James Miller and the girl he was with. Several times James was looking her way too at the same time and smiled. David and Ellie noticed this and they sensed there was more than just casual friendship here.

The taffy was pulled and worked and twisted like long ropes until it was a golden brown color. There was much small talk and laughing as the busy hands worked.

When everything was finished and the candy was ready for eating, several girls helped Mrs. Eash clean up while the others placed songbooks and chairs for the time of singing.

Dishes of the taffy were put at convenient places on the table and sideboard so everyone could help themselves. Mr. Eash had a few boys help him carry benches down from the upstairs for more seating.

Now the singing began. Becky was aware, right away, of a deep bass voice blending in with the rest of the youth. She looked across the room and saw it was James Miller's voice. She also saw that Sam and some of his buddies were making fun of him. But, if James noticed, he evidently didn't let it bother him. He sang with gusto. The Amish sing only the melody, no parts. Becky thought it sounded beautiful to hear a deep bass. Susan began to sing alto, and Rebecca could have listened forever.

But now Sam devised a plan to confuse James.

"*Buwe* (boys)," he said to his corner of rowdies, "let's choose a German song for our next selection. He won't know the words, so that ought to stop him." The others laughed boisterously. Just the thought of Sam Lapp leading a hymn, and a German one at that, made them laugh. But to call James Miller's bluff—that was too good to let pass.

"We'll show that little *Grutze* (cob)," Sam remarked with a sneer.

Sure enough, when the words of the last line died away, Sam Lapp surprised everyone by saying, "Page four hundred and thirty-eight, in the back of the book."

Becky knew the German songs were in that part of the book and wondered why Sam was taking such interest in the singing. *He must be trying to impress me or my parents now*, thought Becky. *I just can't believe it*. Neither could any of the other young folks. But it wasn't long before she knew he wasn't sincere. He giggled so, when he started to sing, that David took over and led out. James and Susan just sat quietly until the end of the song.

David Eash looked directly at the boys who had caused the commotion and said, "Let's think of the words we are singing and who we are singing to."

The scheme had backfired, and Sam did not like it at all. He, and those with him, got up and went outside.

Becky was embarrassed. Why did he have to act like that in front of James and Susan? They might think most Amish are like that. Still, she felt sure they could see that her many other friends were nice Christian people.

The evening's activities came to a close all too soon.

As her guests left, Rebecca followed them out on the porch and bade them come again. James and his sister were among the last to leave.

"We had a really good time, Becky," Susan told her friend.

"Yes, we did," James agreed. "Thanks so much for inviting us. I'd like to see our young folks mix more."

"I'll just bet he would," Sam Lapp told his friends.

They were waiting outside for just such a chance to talk to James.

"Say James," Sam began, "can we talk to you a minute? We're sorry for our actions. Us boys decided we want to go snipe hunting tonight yet and we sure would like for you to come along." He kept a straight face, as did the other boys.

"Well, I really should be getting on home. Tomorrow is a busy day for us and I've never hunted snipe before. Maybe I'd just be in the way," he answered.

"Oh no, you wouldn't be in the way," Sam assured him.

"But I don't even have a gun," James informed them.

"*Ach*, you don't need a gun," said Sam. "We need someone to stay by Keller's Pond near the woods and hold the bag. When we chase them out of the woods, they will run into the bag for hiding. Then you close it real quick."

"But I need to walk my sister home. I wouldn't like for

her to go alone after dark."

"You go on if you want to," Susan told him. She and Becky were listening from the porch. The girls had never heard of snipe hunting, either, but it sounded like fun.

"You take your sister home first," Sam offered. "In fact, us boys will walk with you and we can all go from there. It's along the way to Keller's Pond anyhow. Maybe we could borrow a gunny sack from you."

"Well, all right," James agreed, and they said good-bye to Rebecca and went on their way.

"Did you have a good time tonight?" David asked his daughter.

"Yes, I did. All except for what Sam Lapp and those other rowdies did. Dad, what are snipes, and why do people hunt them?" she asked.

David began to chuckle.

"Why do you ask?" he questioned.

"Sam and his friends told James they are sorry for what they did, so they invited him to go along to hunt snipe," she finished.

David laughed some more.

"Rebecca," he said, "there are no such things as snipes. James will be left sitting at the edge of the woods all night, holding that bag. That is, unless he gets wise to them and goes home. That's what they will do once they have him and the bag waiting by the pond. They will leave him to the mosquitoes and damp night air and go home." David kept laughing.

"I don't think it's funny," Becky's temper flared.

"It's an old trick," her dad told her.

"I don't care if it's old or new. It's hateful," Becky ranted.

"Why? Rebecca, is it because it's played on James? If it were played on Sam, would it still be hateful?" her dad put her on the spot.

"He would deserve it," she answered, as she headed for the stairway.

She just wanted to be left alone.

12
The Diary

Rebecca had trouble finding steady work for the winter. It was not nearly as busy a time for the women folk, now that gardening and canning were over with. Unless she could find a family who needed someone for several weeks while the lady of the house was recuperating from childbearing, she would be without work. Becky did not want to depend on her parents. If she kept paying room and board, her savings would dwindle fast.

Things were going better for her at church since her accident. She had not been able to go with the young folks for quite some time. So, since she hadn't been seen with James Miller, she was welcomed back. There were those who would remain her friends regardless, but some felt she was betraying the church and its doctrines.

One Sunday after the biweekly worship service at a home, Enos Plank's wife asked Becky if she could talk with her privately. Becky followed her to the washhouse, where the ladies had left their outer wraps.

There were a few small girls playing in the washhouse,

and an older lady was getting her shawl and bonnet, preparing to leave. Not everyone stayed for the meal that was always served after services.

"Brrr, it's cold out here," Becky exclaimed.

"Yes, it is cold," agreed Lucy Plank, "but I didn't know where we could find a place to be alone. You little girls had better run inside or put your *Mondlin* on." She directed her remark to the two girls now standing watching her and Becky. (A *Mondlin* is a dark-colored cape worn across the shoulders, wrapped around to below the knees, and fastened with matching dark buttons. Small children wear this garment until the girls are old enough to wear shawls and the boys to wear plain coats.)

"You could catch a bad cold," Lucy warned the children. They just looked at her shyly and left. But the minute they thought they were out of hearing range, the two began to giggle as though something funny had happened. However, they did go into the warm house. The older lady who had come for her wraps finally left also, sensing Lucy and Rebecca wanted to be alone.

"Becky," Lucy began right away, "I will need a *Maut* in March. Has anyone asked you for that time?"

"No, they haven't," Becky gladly assured her.

"I'll need you at least four weeks. Could you stay that long?" asked Lucy.

"As far as I know now. Anyway, I won't promise anybody else," Becky said.

"Good," answered Lucy, and that was all that was said. No wages were discussed at all. Becky just assumed she would get the customary three-fifty a week plus bed and board. The Plank's had five children and the oldest one was a boy of eight. There would be a lot to do, but she was not afraid of hard work. She knew that a reputation for being a good worker would be an important qualification for being a good wife.

Rebecca was an excellent *Maut* and so she did find short-term work a few weeks at one place and then she was home for several weeks and someone else would want her for a "Baby Case," as the women put it.

One evening she had just helped her mother finish the supper dishes when there was a knock at the door.

"See who it is, David," Ellie called to her husband.

"Oh, come on in," Becky heard her father say. Then he said, "Becky, it's Susan. I guess she wants to see you."

Becky quickly welcomed her friend, and Susan could tell she was glad to see her.

"Susan, I'm so happy you came. But didn't you about freeze walking down here? It's sure cold out," she said.

"No, I kept warm because I walked so fast and even ran part of the way. The cold couldn't catch up with me," she laughed.

"How are your folks, Susan?" asked Ellie.

"Oh, real good. Mom had strep throat about three weeks ago, but she is fine again. And what about your family?"

"We can't complain. Other than the sniffles and aches and pains of growing older, we have been well."

They talked of things such as weddings in the community, new babies, farm sales, families who were moving, and so on.

"Let's go upstairs to my room, Susan," Becky invited her. "I have something to show you."

"It's likely to be pretty chilly up there, Becky," her mother warned. "Maybe you had better light the little kerosene heater and take it along. Be sure to open the floor register."

"*Ach*, Mom," answered Becky, "you are like a mother hen. We will be all right. I will open the register and wear my shawl. Susan can keep her coat on until the room warms up a bit."

"What do you want to show me?" Susan asked curiously as soon as they entered Becky's room.

Throwing her shawl around her shoulders and opening the register, Becky stepped over to her dresser. She took a box out of a drawer, removed its cover, and held it out for her friend to see. It was a beautiful olive green diary with gold trim.

"Oh, it's beautiful," Susan exclaimed. "Where did you get it?"

Becky's face flushed slightly, but she answered, "It came in the mail last Tuesday. I had no idea who would be sending me a present so long after my accident."

"Well, who?" asked Susan, almost bursting to know. "Who was it?"

"Your brother," Becky replied, blushing again.

"My brother!" exclaimed Susan. "James?"

"Yes, James," Becky said. "And I don't know why. Why would he send something to me?"

"Well, Becky, I know he thinks a lot of you," Susan told her.

"Oh, Susan, he shouldn't have. I think he is a nice boy, too, but he should not send me presents."

"Why not?" Susan wondered. "What's wrong with that?"

"Nothing—I don't know—it's just that—well—" Becky stuttered.

"Do you mean it's because he isn't Amish, Rebecca?" her friend asked.

"No, oh no, Susan! Please don't think that. To me it doesn't matter if he isn't, but some people will talk and find fault," Becky told her.

"So that's it. You do like my brother, but you are afraid of what people will say if they knew it. Becky, we all have to live our own life. We don't try to please everybody. It can't be done. Pray for God's leading and then live to

97

please him and him alone. Not even yourself."

"Susan, you are so smart. I wish I knew all the answers like you and James do," Rebecca remarked.

"Oh, Becky, we don't know nearly all we need to know. We are still learning and always will be. Did James write anything with your gift explaining why he sent it?" asked Susan.

"He only wrote 'To a Friend, I hope you like this gift.' That's all," Becky replied. "What should I do? Should I keep it, Susan? It's not my birthday or anything."

"Do you like the diary, Becky?"

"Of course I do. I like it a lot," Becky told Susan.

"Well then, keep it. Do you want me to tell James you got it all right and that you like it?"

"Yes, and thank him for me too, will you please?"

"Sure," Susan promised. "Now I'll tell you my reason for coming tonight."

"I'm sorry," Becky apologized, "I did not mean to talk about myself all evening and leave you out."

"This is about you too, Becky," Susan said. "Here is what I wanted to talk about with you. You see, I know you don't have any steady work, just several weeks now and then, so I have a place in town where there is a good opportunity, if you are strong enough to work regular and want it."

"Is this the same place you asked me about once before? Remember? The one you mentioned the night of the box social?" Becky asked.

"That's the one. The doctor's wife is spending more time at the office, helping him with appointments and paper work. They really need someone. They have two children, both in school. In the summer, they are at summer camp or visiting grandparents. It sounds like such an easy place to work. They are Christian people, which means a lot. The pay would be forty dollars a week."

"Forty!" Becky sat upright with a start. Never had she heard of such exuberant wages. "Did you say forty a week?"

"Yes, I did. That's what they said they would pay. And being Christian, I'm sure they keep their word."

"Do you know what that comes to for one month? One hundred and sixty dollars! Oh, Susan, I want it! Really I do. Would they still come and get me Monday mornings and bring me home Friday afternoons?" Becky asked.

"As far as I know. I'm sure they would. Then shall I tell them you can start right away?"

"Yes, tell them—," but then Becky remembered. "Oh no!" she exclaimed.

"Becky, what's wrong?" asked Susan. "Why do you look so frightened?"

"*Ach*, Susan, I almost forgot. I can't work for the doctor and his wife. I promised Enos Planks to help out when their baby arrives," she answered despairingly.

"How soon is that?" Susan asked.

"In March. And next week is the first of the month. I told her I can stay four weeks. Oh, why did I promise? I'll only get three-fifty a week."

"Maybe we can still work out something," Susan said hopefully. "Why don't I ask Mr. and Mrs. Feltman if they could wait until the first of April. If they want an Amish or Mennonite girl badly enough, they will make it until then, I'm sure."

"Oh, Susan, could you find out? It all sounds so wonderful," Becky said enthusiastically.

But after Susan left for home and Becky was alone with her thoughts, she didn't know if it was such a good idea after all. What would her parents say? She knew it was thought best for the Amish girls to work among their own people, to avoid the temptations found in many English homes. Therefore, she was surprised to hear the response of both her parents when she related the news to them one morning at breakfast.

"Mom, Dad," she began, "I think after I'm finished working for the Planks, I may take a job in town for a doctor and his wife. It's still a little difficult for me to do real hard work since my accident and the pay would be much better, too. Then I could pay you more room and board."

"You haven't heard us complain about boarding you, now did you?" asked her dad.

"No, but I just don't want to be a burden," she answered.

"We will tell you when that happens, old granny," her father teased. Then he said, "Rebecca, your mother and I feel you are old enough and have been taught well enough to know what's right. So, if you want to work for English folks, we trust you to keep within the rules of the church. Do what you think is best."

Everything seemed right again. She would not let her parents down. That evening, she opened the diary that James had sent to her and made her first entry.

This is what she wrote:

Dear Diary,
    Today my parents made me very happy. They have proved they trust me. I shall be working in town for English people. Help me to never disappoint Mom and Dad or God. I'm so happy.

13
Home Cures

Becky saw the buggy pull in the drive and recognized Mr. Plank as soon as he got out and tied his horse to the hitching post. She had been helping Ellie tear carpet rags, which her mother would weave on her loom and sell for a little extra pin money.

"I'd better go upstairs and pack my suitcase *schnell* (quickly)," Becky told her mom. "Here comes Enos Plank and I can guess why."

Enos opened the door and called out, "*Sind deah daheem* (are you home)?" Enos felt such kinship with a fellow Amish family that he didn't bother to knock.

Ellie replied, "*Kumm yuscht rei* (just come in)."

"Well, I came for my *Maut*," Enos stated. "Can you come right away?" He directed his question to Rebecca.

"Just as soon as I get packed," she answered him.

"What do you have this time?" asked Ellie.

"A little dishwasher. That gives us three dishwashers and three wood choppers," he said with satisfaction.

Becky made her way upstairs to get her things ready to

leave for her next place of employment.

She had just left the room when David came in from thawing some pipes at the watering trough.

"*Wie geht's* (how do you do), Enos? I thought that looked like your rig. Well, I suppose you came for a *Maut.* Here, sit down while you wait. You know how long it takes these women to get ready to go some place," and he looked at Ellie with that grin he always had when he was teasing. Enos just chuckled as he took the chair David offered him.

"Looks like we are in for some more cold weather. I heard it thunder in the empty woods night before last and it sure turned cold again," Enos said. By empty woods he meant the trees bare of leaves.

"Well now, that's a new one on me," David remarked, "I never heard that before."

"Oh, my grandfather told us that way back already. It's true, too. You just pay attention once and you will find out."

They talked of crop prices as well as milk and egg sales. Mrs. Eash asked how Lucy Plank and the new baby were doing and what they had named the young miss. Enos assured her everyone was fine, but as for naming the babies, that was his wife's department. Ellie thought this rather strange, as she and David had shared in naming their children.

Becky soon had her suitcase ready and told Enos she could leave anytime.

"I may need to keep her this first Sunday, if she can stay," he said, more to Ellie than anyone.

"That's up to Becky," her mother said.

"Yes, I'll stay Sunday, if you need me," she told Enos.

"Well, then we had better get going. Mom has a neighbor staying with her until we get home. Don't work too hard, David," his friend said as he went out the door.

Enos Plank was a friendly person, easy to talk with. He took Becky's suitcase and carried it to the buggy, depositing it in the rear box. Then closing and snapping the curtain on her side, he untied his horse, climbed in, closed the curtain on his side and started them on their way. The buggies in the area where Becky lived were black in color. The leather curtains would roll up in the warm weather and be fastened with snaps to hold them in place. But in winter weather, they were let down and closed with snaps on the edge of the opening for warmth. They had glass fronts with small openings in the box below the glass for the reins (lines) to be pulled through in order to guide the horse. Enos and Becky visited pleasantly all the way to the Plank homestead.

"Here we are," Enos said, turning in the driveway.

"My, it seems we just left my place," Becky commented.

Enos pulled to the front gate and stopped. Becky waited until he got out and undid the curtain on her side. Enos reached in and got her suitcase from the back buggy box and said, "Just go in the front door." He led his horse and buggy toward the buggy shed and Becky was left on her own.

She picked up her heavy suitcase and started toward the house. Little faces peered at her from the kitchen windows. *Five children*, she thought! Opening the front door, she stepped inside. As she always did when she began a new place of work, she wondered what this one would be like.

The neighbor lady came bustling in from the living room to greet her. "Chust come in and make yourself at home," she invited Becky. She had a very definite German accent. Becky liked her right away. She looked so motherly and cheerful. "Put your suitcase here by the stairway and come see the new *Bobbli* (baby). *Ach*, she is so small."

Becky deposited her suitcase in the place suggested and followed the elderly lady to the bedroom. Mrs. Plank lay there in bed with the little bundle in her arms.

"Oh, let me see her," Becky gurgled. "Look at that head of hair. Why, I don't believe I've ever seen a baby with such a head full."

"*Ach* vel," was Lucy Plank's reply. She was not much for fuss or flattery. Turning to her neighbor lady, she said, "You can go on home now. Enos can take you if you want."

"No, I can walk," her friend said. "It will be good for my *Speck* (fat)." She laughed heartily and, telling Lucy to take good care of herself, she went for her wraps.

Mrs. Plank's relatives all had to come and see the new *Bobbli;* so also did many friends and neighbors. Each one of the women seemed to have some word of advice for Lucy. *You would think it was her first one,* Becky remarked to herself.

"Mind now, you stay in bed a full ten days and the tenth day lay real still," her Aunt Beverly told her. "The tenth day is the most crucial one. That's when everything comes back in its place again."

Becky's week was a very busy one. Two-year-old Emma was afraid of strangers and cried whenever Becky changed her. She stayed close by her mother's bedside most of the time. Often she tried to climb up on the bed. But Rebecca Eash gradually won the heart of the little miss by her patient loving ways. In three days time, she was toddling around after Becky wherever she went.

One day, little Emma and her four-year-old brother were in the living room playing when Lucy called Becky to check on them.

"I believe they're into something, maybe. I heard them laughing and Alva was saying, '*Geh, muck* (go, fly).'"

Rebecca investigated and found, to her amusement,

Alva with the sewing machine oilcan and a well-oiled fly. He was trying to get the fly to crawl up the window. Not yet warmed by the morning sun, the fly was sluggish and the little boy wanted to help him along.

"What are you doing?" asked Becky.

"*Eeling de Muck* (oiling the fly)."

Laughing, Becky took the oilcan from the grimy little hand. She put it high on the mantle shelf, out of reach of curious children. After washing Alva's hands and face, she disposed of the unlucky fly and cleaned the window and surrounding sill. When she told Lucy what her son was up to, they both laughed.

"*Ach* my," said Lucy, "what those little ones don't get into."

Sunday brought a lot of company to the Plank family. Rebecca had cleaned and baked all Saturday in preparation. Then, of course, that evening was bath night. The old tin tub was brought into the kitchen after supper and one by one the children were scrubbed clean. Becky washed and braided little Emma's hair. Then she tied a scarf on her head so she wouldn't get *schtrublich* (hair messed up). This would have to last for a week. Between washings and braidings, Emma's hair would be smoothed back under her little black cap.

After everyone else had bathed, including the man of the house, Becky prepared warm clean water and, making sure the kitchen was deserted, she had her chance to clean up. How refreshed she felt as she climbed between the soft blankets and relaxed for a good night of sleep.

One of the families that spent Sunday afternoon with Enos and Lucy Plank was a young couple with their first child, a little girl, possibly nine months old. The baby was so fussy and cried almost all the while they were visiting.

"Is your baby cutting teeth?" Lucy asked the young woman.

"I don't think so," answered the distraught mother. "She just got two new ones this past week. It seems the last two months she has done a lot of crying. We have had her to the doctor several times, but it seems he can't find anything wrong with her."

This started a whole deluge of conversation and advice among the women.

"Sounds to me as if she might have pinworms," said Sevilla Yoder. "My Susie had them when she was two and she was fussy day and night until I treated her with a bit of kerosene and sugar."

"Yuck, I'd hate to give that to my baby," commented Lucy.

"I know what I'm talking about and it helped." Sevilla told them.

"Well, it sounds to me like she may have stomach trouble or fever." Mrs. Yutzy offered her opinion.

"Or it could be weight loss. Her milk may not be right for her. Have you tried other milk?"

"I've tried several different kinds. In fact, I've tried just about everything," answered Ada Frey, the child's mother.

"If I were you, Ada," began Lydia Yutzy, "I'd *brauch* (powwow) for her. You can do what you want, but it has helped mine many times."

Becky's curiosity was aroused as soon as she heard powwow mentioned. She had been passing a bowl of apples to the visitors, and just entered the bedroom where the women were having this discussion. She listened intently. *Now,* she thought, *I will hear more about this mysterious method.*

"Well," said Ada, "I've never seen how you do it and I don't know how to powwow, but I'm ready to learn and willing to try most anything."

Mrs. Yutzy smiled and said, "Not everyone can *brauch,*

but I've done it and, if you want, we can do it right here."

"You mean now?" asked the astonished mother.

"Sure, if you want to," answered Lydia.

"Guess it wouldn't hurt to try," Ada Frey told her. "Let's do it then."

"You have to believe it will help though," her friend said. "I will need a piece of string and a raw egg. Tell Enos not to put any coals on the fire for I need a smoldering heat."

"Becky, will you go tell Enos that and also bring some string from the sewing machine drawer and a raw egg?" Lucy told her *Maut.*

Rebecca had been standing in amazement as she listened. Now she left the room, gave Enos the message, and brought the two items. She watched as Lydia took the string and measured the baby around the waist, then its length and its width. Next, she wrapped the string around the egg. Opening the stove, she placed the egg onto the live coals. If the egg popped loudly, the powwow took and the child would be much better.

Just to make sure they were powwowing for the right thing, they also did it for the cure of not gaining weight as she should. For this they took the squirming child, who cried loudly for her mother, and passed her from Lydia to Sevilla, underneath the table and around the table leg a number of times. Becky noticed Lydia's lips move, but she could not hear what she was saying. *Is it about "the green olive tree?"* she wondered. Mrs. Frey took her crying child, thanked Lydia and Sevilla, then told her husband she was ready to go home. Becky went about her duties, but she felt she must find out more about this unusual custom.

14
Out for Ice Cream

"Here's a letter for you, Rebecca," Enos told her, handing a blue envelope to his hired girl.

"For me!" she exclaimed. "Who would be writing to me?"

"Oh, who knows, with all the handsome boys around," Enos teased.

"Oh, you men! Always teasing," Becky said as she glanced at the return address. "Why, it's from Susan," she said happily. "See there, it isn't from a fellow. I told her I'd be working here. Wonder what she wants, or why she would be writing to me?"

"Only one way to find out," Enos said. "Open it," and he laughed again.

"I know that," Becky answered, but before she got that far, little Emma dropped a glass of milk and needed attention. The letter would have to wait.

After Rebecca had cleaned up the spilled milk, Alva came crying with a stubbed toe. She cleaned and bandaged that. Alva never liked wearing shoes and, despite repeated paddlings, he often ran around in his stockings or even his bare feet in cold weather.

"Maybe that will help you remember to wear your shoes when Mom tells you to," Lucy told her young son. "See, now you have an ouchie. Stop crying and dry the dishes for Becky. I think she would like some help."

Becky really could do the dishes quicker by herself, but Amish children learn to help at an early age. She handed Alva a clean dish towel and prepared the warm sudsy water in the large dishpan for washing. Alva was still crying softly as he took the towel. Becky saw a tear clinging to his eyelash. It freed itself and made its way down the chubby cheek to the trembling little chin. Becky's heart melted.

"Want to play a guessing game while we work?" she asked.

Alva paused uncertainly for a brief moment. Then his little face brightened and smiling, he said, "*Ya,* I want."

"I'll start," Becky told him. "Now, I see something in this room that is red. Can you guess what it is?" Alva guessed several things, but finally spied his winter cap on its hook inside the entranceway and said with confidence, "*Tsipple Kapp.*"

"That's right," laughed Becky. "It's your turn."

So the game went on, and at times Rebecca pretended she could not guess what Alva saw. This delighted the little boy and, before he realized it, the dishes were done. Even the sore toe was forgotten. Alva did not know it, but Becky was also using this method to teach him the basic colors. *What a good* Maut *she is,* thought Lucy Plank. *I shall surely miss her when she leaves us. She will make someone a lovely wife.*

The letter that had come for Becky lay on the shelf of the buffet until after supper. When her day's work was finished, Rebecca snatched it from the shelf and hurried upstairs. Quickly she lit the kerosene lamp, grabbed her shawl for warmth, and sat on the edge of the bed. Her hands trembled as she opened the envelope. Earlier, she had felt a bit miffed at all the interruptions, which kept her from reading its contents. But forgetting all that, her eyes began to scan the page.

> Dear Becky,
>
> I have good news for you. Last evening, I had a chance to see Mrs. Feltman, the doctor's wife, and I told her your predicament. She informed me that there is no problem. She will wait until you are finished working at your present job. Just think, Becky, we will be able to call each other on the telephone. I have such nice people to work for, too. Oh, I'm so excited.
>
> By the way, I told James you liked his gift and that you told me to thank him. He said he is glad you like it. Besides, he would like to come see you this Saturday night, so don't be surprised if he shows up on your doorstep. Maybe you could tell James then how soon you could come to work for Mrs. Feltman and I'll let her know.
>
> Looking forward to seeing you soon.
>
> > Your friend,
> > Susan

Becky's heart was pounding. *It's just because I'll be working in town,* she tried to convince herself. And forty dollars a week! But she knew better. Rebecca Eash knew why her pulse was racing. James wanted to come and see her. She was glad, and still she didn't want to cause hurt feelings again. She loved a peaceful life. What was it Susan had told her? Oh, now she remembered. *Don't try to please everyone, not even yourself. Live to please God.* With these thoughts, she blew out the light and knelt a long time by her bedside in prayer.

Sometimes when Amish girls work as hired girls in other Amish homes they help outside almost as much, or more, as indoors. In fact, where there are more girls than boys in a family, the *Maut* often helps with the milking, field work, and even cleaning out the cow and horse stalls. But at Enos Plank's, Becky was not asked nor expected to do such tasks. She was grateful.

"Well, Rebecca," Lucy began, "this is now the third week you have been here. Since this is Saturday, I guess we will have you just one more week. You are such a good worker that I'd like to keep you for the summer, but we just can't afford it. I'm thankful that I could have you this long."

"Lucy, I like working for you and Enos," Rebecca told her. "You are nice people and you make your children mind. Some places I've worked were not very easy. The children were left to do as they pleased."

"That is too bad," Lucy answered. "I often think what Proverbs says about a child left to his own way bringing his mother to shame."

"I know some of those mothers were embarrassed by the way their offspring acted, but they didn't do much about it. Of course, I haven't raised a family of my own, so I'd better not talk," Becky said.

"Well, if you do as good as your parents did, I don't think you need to worry. All of your family turned out well and all have stayed Amish. That speaks well for your folks," Lucy concluded.

Becky wished she hadn't made that last statement. *Why is it so important to stay Amish? Aren't Susan and James faithful Christians in the Mennonite church? Perhaps God's love is broader than human minds. Didn't God choose the Jews and yet extend his loving grace in Christ to Gentiles who believe?* She puzzled over these questions in her mind.

"Why are you slicking up so?" David asked Becky.

It was Saturday evening after supper and Rebecca had just come down from changing clothes upstairs.

"Are you going someplace?" her mother now asked.

"No, not that I know of, unless . . . ." She paused.

"Unless what?" David prompted her.

"Oh, Susan wrote me a letter this week and she said James wants to come tonight."

"So," said David, "that again. I like him all right, Rebecca, but I hope it won't stir up trouble."

"I don't know why it should," Becky told him.

"I think you know why it might," Ellie reminded her daughter.

"But Mom, why should I try to live to please everyone else? I don't care how other people choose to do, unless it's against the Bible. And I don't see that being friends with James Miller is unscriptural!" There, she had said it. And if it sounded spunky or disrespectful, she didn't mean it to.

"What have we here, Mother," asked David. "Did you know we raised such a sassy girl?"

"Just be sure you are no more than friends," advised Ellie.

Rebecca wished it were summertime so she could wait on the porch swing until James arrived. Instead, she stayed in the warm living room and chatted with her parents. She told them about little Alva oiling the half-frozen fly and also about the powwowing for Ada Frey's fussy baby. They laughed at her first story but as for the second incident, both of her parents wondered at such practices.

There was a knock at the front door and Becky went to open it.

"Hello, James. Susan wrote and told me you were coming."

"May I come in?" he asked.

"*Ach*, sure," Becky said, "I don't know what I was thinking about, to let you stand here in the cold. Come on into the living room. Mom, Dad," she called, "it's James."

As if they hadn't known. Let it be said that, even though Becky's parents wished she would keep company only with Amish boys, they received James warmly. For that, Becky was truly thankful.

"Come in, James," David invited, and Ellie offered him a chair. They all had a short, pleasant visit, then James said, "If Becky would care to go with me, I wonder if you would object if we went over to Krupper's Korner for some ice cream."

"What do you say, Mom?" David asked his wife.

"I guess it's all right, if you don't come home too late. Tomorrow is our church Sunday, you know." Ellie wanted her daughter to get enough sleep so she could stay awake during the three-hour service on backless benches.

Becky said she would love to go for some ice cream. This time, instead of wearing her shawl and bonnet, she wore a short, waist-length, dark blue coat with snap fasteners and a blue scarf to match.

"Good-bye, Mom and Dad," Becky called back as she started out the door.

"I'll have her home in an hour, at the most," James promised.

"We will be watching the clock," David said with a teasing grin.

"Your dad sure likes to kid people, doesn't he?" James remarked.

"All the time," Becky answered. "But he sure has a lot of friends, and people seem to like both him and my mom."

"I'm sure. I feel the same way about your parents and I like their daughter too," James said.

Oh dear! Becky hadn't expected him to say that, and yet it brought a warm, happy feeling. She was silent.

"Well," said James, trying to keep his eyes and his

113

mind on the road as he drove. "I had hoped you would tell me you care at least a little bit for me too."

"Of course I do," Becky quickly responded, "but it's not—I mean, we wouldn't—it could never—." The more she tried to explain, the more frustrated she became again.

"I know," James said. "I didn't mean to upset you. We will talk about it later. Right now I'd better watch where I'm going," he laughed, as he missed his turn onto Krupper Street. He pulled into the next side street and headed back to the corner.

The little ice-cream parlor was almost deserted and James was glad. Sometimes on a Saturday night, it was filled with young people from various places. They soon found a table and made their selections. James was surprised to learn that Becky had never eaten a banana split before.

"You mean, you never in your life ate a banana split?" James asked in amazement.

"No, I never did," Becky answered.

"What made you order one, then? How did you know you'd like it?"

"Because that's what you said you would get, so I figured it must be good from your description."

"I hope you won't be disappointed," he told her.

Becky wasn't disappointed, but she was embarrassed that James spent so much money for her.

"I should have ordered a cone instead," she told James.

"No way," he said. "A girl like you deserves the best."

Becky blushed, not knowing what to say.

"Rebecca," James began, "I would like to go steady with you, but I know that would cause problems. Do you suppose if I would leave the Mennonite church and join the Amish church, I would be accepted?"

Becky was shocked. "James," she exclaimed, "do you

114

realize what that would mean? Why, you would have to give up so many of your things and your way of life."

"I know, Becky, but for you I will. Somehow I've always felt the Lord is calling me to a special work. Maybe I'll find it with your people."

Rebecca didn't know what to say.

"Take me home, James," she requested.

"I hope I didn't upset you." James spoke out of concern.

"No, I just need to think about this," she answered.

15
Becoming Amish

After Esther's wedding and her move to Iowa with her husband, the *Dawdy Haus* stood empty.

"It just doesn't seem right," fussed Becky's mother.

"Maybe we should rent it out. It would bring a little extra income for you and Dad," Rebecca suggested.

"I had never thought of that, but, yes, maybe that would be good. I'll talk to David about it," she decided.

So that is how it happened that an English family by the name of Rowan moved in. Earl and Debbie Rowan had two children. Mr. Rowan worked in town at the paper mill and they desperately needed a place to live.

"Do you think it's wise to rent to an Englisher?" Ellie asked her husband.

"Mom," he answered, "all I know is he came to me in need and I felt it my duty to help him."

"Well then, it's settled," answered Ellie.

Becky took a liking to the Rowan children immediately. Karen was five and her sister, Nila, was three. Both were blond with long silky hair and blue eyes. They were well-behaved little girls. Becky especially loved to hear them singing little songs they learned in Sunday school. Even though Nila was only three, she would join right in with Karen and they sang from the heart. Her favorite one was "Jewels." As the girls sang, "When he cometh, when he cometh to make up his jewels," Becky thought, *these are two of his precious jewels right here.*

Becky had other thoughts too. Especially about her own life. She had talked to her parents about James joining the Amish church.

Her father had asked her, "Rebecca, do you really believe that's a good reason for him to join?"

"I don't know, Dad," she answered. "Sometimes I'm so *verhuddelt* (mixed-up). I've gone out lots of times with Amish boys. Some are pleasant and some aren't. But there is something different about James. He often talks about the Scriptures and he told me he believes the Lord has a special work for him. He thinks maybe he can find it among our people."

"I don't know, Rebecca," her mother spoke up. "You had better be careful. Some have done this before and it didn't last. They ended up leaving the church after a while."

"Naturally," David remarked, "if this boy is really sincere and wants to live a less worldly life, how can we say no?"

So, day after day, Becky struggled, with her emotions going one direction one day and completely opposite the next. She had finished her work for the Plank family and was now working for Dr. and Mrs. Feltman. They certainly were fine Christian people, just as Susan had told her.

The doctor's wife told Becky one day that her husband never performed surgery without praying first. This impressed Rebecca Eash very much. She wondered how many of her own people practiced this before any major undertaking in their own lives, including herself.

There were so many new gadgets at the Feltman home that an Amish girl was not familiar with and had to learn how to operate. A washer and dryer, electric sweeper, electric can opener, a toaster, and a microwave oven. These were all new to Becky and she wondered if she would be able to learn how to use each one. She was almost afraid to touch some of them. Mrs. Feltman laughed at her caution, but spent most of two weeks "breaking her in," as Becky put it. At the end of the two weeks Rebecca was surprised at how much she had mastered.

Susan and Rebecca used the phone to call each other with their employers' permission, but never abused that privilege. Sometimes, if they finished work early, they were allowed to walk to the ice-cream shop for a cone. Often, they would do the grocery shopping together for their families, as they laughingly referred to them. Susan would take her car and pick up Becky. They were glad their ladies both wanted their purchases made at the same grocery store. Of course, there weren't too many choices with only one large supermarket and two small family-owned places.

One day, as they were shopping, Susan asked Becky a question that startled her.

"Becky," she said, "I thought you and James had been getting along real well and were seeing more of each other lately. What made you change your mind?"

"What do you mean, Susan?"

Her friend saw that Becky was surprised by her question. "Well, I wasn't going to say anything, but James has been so hurt. Why did you write what you did in that letter?"

Now Rebecca was truly in the dark.

"Whatever are you talking about? I didn't write a letter

to your brother."

"Someone sure did," Susan remarked, "and it wasn't very nice. In fact, we couldn't believe you did it. But your name was signed, and how were we to know?"

"Tell me what it said."

Susan hesitated, "Are you sure you want to know?"

"Please tell me," begged Becky.

"Well, it said for James just to get the notion out of his head about joining the Amish church. He would never make an Amishman anyway. He can't even speak the language, let alone know their church rules. Besides, as for that silly notion that God has a special work for him—hogwash! There are plenty of nice Amish boys who would make a better husband. . . ."

"Stop!" exclaimed Becky. "How awful. Does James really think I wrote that?" Dismay was written all over her face.

"No, I don't really think he does, Becky. But it hurts him to know that anyone feels this way about him."

"Oh, I'm so ashamed," Becky confessed. "I don't know if I can ever face your brother again."

"Well, why not? You didn't write it," Susan said.

"No, I certainly didn't. But just to think that one of our people did—and I believe I may know who," she concluded.

"Really, Becky? How can you know?" Susan questioned her.

"I don't want to blame someone innocent, but Sam Lapp asked me for a date last year. I didn't want to go with him, but I had told him no so many times that I felt perhaps I wasn't fair to him. Well, Susan, it was absolutely the worst date I've ever had. If he wasn't bragging on himself or running James down, he was trying to kiss me. I was disgusted and told him I did not care to go out with him again—ever!"

"Oh, Becky, I know what you mean. We have some Mennonite boys who think they are God's gift to women. But we also have some sensible and kind young men."

"Same with our Amish boys. Most are real decent, but Sam Lapp is definitely not one of them. I probably shouldn't have told him that James is concerned to find God's special plan for his life; he does know about that. Oh, Susan, what should I do?" Becky asked again.

"I'll tell James you did not write that letter. That, in itself, will help a lot. Should I tell him you suspect who did write it?"

"That's up to you, Susan but if I know Sam Lapp, he won't be able to keep his mouth shut and will have to find out if James got the letter," Becky surmised.

A few weeks later the young folks were having a baseball game, Maple View Mennonite against the Amish youth. This brought James and Sam face to face when Sam hit a double. James was playing second base.

"Guess this shows you Mennonites us Amish can play ball," Sam boasted.

"That was a good hit, Sam," agreed James.

"Say, James," Sam asked, "did you get any letters lately?"

Just then the crack of the bat sent the ball flying out to right field. Before James could answer, Sam was off and running. It may have been just as well because James was fighting the temptation to give Sam a few sharp words. The outfielder caught the ball and threw Sam out at home plate, which he tried to make against the advice of his teammates.

He argued with the umpire, then threw his hat on the ground and, with a beet-red face, walked off the field.

He's got a temper he can't hold either, James noted to himself. Now he knew who had sent that letter, for they had told no one.

Rebecca was right.

When Becky told her parents about the letter Sam Lapp had written, they too were shocked.

"A person can get in trouble for forging someone's name," David told his daughter.

"*Ach*, Dad, I don't want to get him into trouble. I just wish he could accept James as a friend and, before long, as a fellow church member," Becky answered David.

James had made application to join the Amish church. He had to take instruction sessions every other Sunday and, as the minister said, "Prove himself."

This meant he had better not be caught driving his or any car. He must wear broadfall pants and plain clothes. His hair had to be a certain length and a certain cut. It looked like a bowl had been placed on his head and the hair cut around it. The Sunday before he would be taken into the church, he must not shave his whiskers. After he became a member, he would be clean shaven again until he became a married man. From then he must wear a beard.

He and Becky were now "going steady," and Rebecca often asked him if he was sure he would not regret becoming Amish.

"We'll have to wait and see," he would tease her. "I'm not Amish yet." But then, seriously, he would assure her he felt this was the Lord's leading. He prayed often about it and, unless he could plainly see a different way, this was it.

Becky accepted that, but she knew he missed not going to church every Sunday, Sunday evening, and midweek Bible study. Once, she mentioned this to him and he said, "Becky. I see no reason why we can't study the Bible and pray together on the in-between Sunday and Sunday evening and Wednesday evening too. Besides, that would give me more reason to come oftener." He grinned, and Rebecca liked the idea. Hardest of all for James was to learn the Amish language.

Becky tried to teach him in that too, and many times they laughed at his pronunciation. But he tried, and she was a willing teacher.

Some words in the Amish dialect sound almost alike but have a completely different meaning. Such as *Gaul* (horse) and *Gall* (gallon).

One Sunday evening, James was helping with chores at the Eash home. He told Ellie that the water fountain in the hen house must have been almost empty for he put a whole *Gaul* (horse) in it and it still wasn't full. When everyone laughed, he asked what he said wrong, and then joined heartily in their fun. This was another thing Becky admired him for. He could laugh at himself.

The Sunday James was to become a member of the Amish church, his parents and Susan also attended. Some of his brothers and quite a number of his Mennonite friends could not understand his way of thinking. But most wished him well.

Before the preaching and worship service, James met with the ministers in an upstairs room, which had been made ready beforehand. There were six chairs where they sat until such a time as they were satisfied that James was ready to be taken into their membership.

There was one problem. The ministers would have liked for James to promise to remain a faithful member of the Amish church as long as he lived. He said he intended to remain faithful as long as he was a member. For, as he put it, "Who knows what life will bring?" At this point and time, he desired to be a member. Usually this would not have passed, but the hand of God must have intervened and James Miller became one with them that day.

16
Our People

Everybody just knew that Rebecca Eash and James Miller were going to get married now. Everybody that is, except Rebecca Eash and James Miller. They enjoyed each other's company, but had never discussed marriage.

Becky was busy working at her place in town. On her Saturdays at home, she often did sewing for herself, pleated coverings (which the Amish wear as prayer veilings), and helped her mother around the house. Mrs. Rowan and her little girls sometimes helped in the garden and with yard work.

"They are a real Christian family and true friends if ever I saw any," Ellie told Rebecca one day. "There just isn't anything they wouldn't do for us. They always take us along to town or to the doctor. We hardly use the buggy anymore, except to go to church."

"That's one thing I still wonder about," Becky said. "You say they are Christian and yet they own a car. So if they are Christian, then you can own a car and not be sinning, right?"

"*Ach*, Becky, I thought you were over this questioning everything. You see, they weren't born Amish. Don't you suppose we were to be Amish or we wouldn't have been born into Amish families?" Ellie reasoned.

"Well," Becky replied, "does that mean that James wasn't meant to be Amish since he wasn't born into an Amish home?"

"No, I didn't mean that."

"Mom, I'm glad I was born into this Amish family. You and Dad love us so much. And with all our friends and relatives, I have a secure feeling. But I think it's even more important to be born again, as Jesus says, and be part of God's family, with a group of Christians who study the Bible."

"Is James dissatisfied already with being Amish?" Ellie asked.

"No, Mom, he hasn't said one word about not being content."

"Well then, if he is happy this way and not being raised Amish, I'm sure you should be."

"Do the Rowans still like living in the *Dawdy Haus*?" asked Becky.

"Oh, they say they miss the electricity. Especially the lights. But they were just happy to find this place."

"Yeah, I guess they needed it pretty badly."

Becky was at work at the Felton's one day, cleaning out the refrigerator, when the telephone rang. Since she was there all alone, she answered it.

"Oh, hello, Susan," she said, hearing her friend's voice.

"Becky, did you hear what happened last night?"

Becky detected alarm in Susan's tone.

"No," she answered, "what happened?"

"Well, I had the radio on here while I was dusting and a news flash came on about a robbery at the North End Service Station. The owner discovered the break-in this morning, and someone phoned a tip to the police. They caught the robbers—and guess what? They were two boys from our own Mennonite church, Willy Damon and Freeman Kalp, and Sam Lapp."

"Oh no!" Becky said. "Won't they ever learn? Susan, I feel sorry for the parents, but I feel more so for the boys."

"So do I," her friend agreed.

"Where are the boys now, Susan?"

"They're in the county jail, waiting to be tried."

"It just goes to show, there are good and bad among us all," Becky told her.

"That's so true," Susan answered. "Oh, and by the way, Becky, Sam Lapp got a car and that's the one they were driving."

"Sam got a car! He got a car!" Becky said emphatically. "After the way he talked to me about going out with boys who own cars. Oh! I'll never understand him. Susan, pray for me that I might have a right attitude toward him. After that date I had with him, and since he wrote that letter to James and signed my name, I've had a real struggle to forgive and forget. So please pray."

"I will," promised Susan. "I know it's not easy to overcome such things, but God is faithful and, if we commit our way to him, he will bring it to pass."

"Thank you, Susan, and thanks for calling. We will both pray for these three boys, and their families too."

"There are broken hearts for sure because of this and I know prayers are needed. Well, good-bye, Becky. I'd better get back to work. I'll let you know if I hear more," promised Susan, and then she hung up.

All afternoon Becky couldn't think of much else other than what Susan had told her. How awful! What a poor testimony to those who were not Christian. What a reproach to the name of Christianity!

"I'm home, Rebecca," called Mrs. Feltman as she came

125

through the foyer. "Is the doctor home yet?" she asked.

"No, not yet," Becky answered.

"Well then, I think he must have been delayed at the hospital. He was called over for an emergency. I'm taking a good shower and, if he isn't home by then, I'll watch some TV. Could you hold dinner until later? I hate to ask you, but I always like to sit down to dinner with my family."

"Oh, that won't be any problem," Becky assured her. "I don't mind."

What a lovely girl she is, thought Mrs. Feltman. *She never complains.*

Mrs. Feltman switched on the TV set and settled back to enjoy the news. Her hired girl was finishing the dessert for dinner (which Becky and the Amish call supper).

"Rebecca, come here quick," she heard her employer call. "Look," she exclaimed, as she pointed to the TV. "Do you know these boys? It says they are Amish and Mennonite."

"Yes," answered Rebecca, hanging her head in shame and blushing deeply. There they were, all three boys, being questioned by the police.

"I can't believe this! I thought your people were such gentle, honest folks," the doctor's wife told her.

"I'm very sorry," Becky said. "Many of our people do live quiet and peaceful lives, but we have problems and struggles same as anyone else. Sometimes they get the better of folks."

"Oh, I didn't mean to blame you personally, for it certainly isn't your fault. It's just, well, I've never heard of something like this among Amish people."

If only Sam Lapp and his two buddies could know the bad name they were giving the Mennonites and Amish.

Becky heard the car pull into the garage and soon the doctor called, "I'm home." She also heard his wife's reply,

"I'm in the den, dear."

Rebecca knew what their conversation would be, but she hoped they would say no more to her about the situation. It wasn't to be. Doctor Feltman asked her, as soon as he came to the dining room, whether she knew a Sam Lapp. She told him she did.

"I was called over to the hospital," he said, "because the owner of the North End Station was upset over the robbery and publicity and had a heart attack this evening. That's why I'm late. I understand some of your boys did it. It just amazed me, because I've never heard of anything like this before from your people."

As embarrassed as she was, Becky wished he wouldn't say your people. That seemed to make her guilty with the culprits.

"I'm sorry," she said softly. "It should never have happened and I'm sure the parents of the boys and the whole community are sad because of it." She had to fight tears as she spoke.

"May I please be excused? I'm not very hungry," she asked the lady of the house. "I'll bring dessert in when you are ready," Becky said.

"I hope we didn't upset you," Mrs. Feltman said. "We certainly did not mean to."

"That's all right," Rebecca answered. "I'm just not hungry."

"Stella," began the doctor, after Becky left the room. "Do you suppose Rebecca might be related to one of those boys? You know, cousin or perhaps stepbrother. The Amish seem to be related to everyone in some way," he concluded.

"It could be," his wife answered. "I hope she understands that we did not mean to be critical, but that this is very unusual and that's why we were so amazed."

"Rebecca seems to be a sensible girl," answered Bill

Feltman, "and I think she understands."

It was always nice to get back home Friday afternoon, even though Becky thoroughly enjoyed her work for the doctor and his family. She especially loved the Sundays and holidays when her brothers and sisters would come with their families. There were numerous nieces and nephews now, too. Often, after a good, hearty meal, they would all gather around and sing those old songs so dear to their hearts. Even the little ones helped as well as they could.

The renters of the *Dawdy Haus* were invited over for singing many times and joined right in—except for the German songs. For those, they would just hum along. James also did not know German well enough to participate. He tried so hard to learn the language and, more than once, he would laugh along with the rest when he made a mistake. Rebecca's heart went out to him. Whenever he came for her with his horse and buggy, instead of the warm car he used to drive, she would ask him, "Don't you miss your car? It was so much easier for you. You didn't have to hitch the horse to the buggy and drive longer to get here."

"But just think," he would respond, "the tank is never almost empty, and I need not check the oil or fix a flat tire." James laughed, but Rebecca thought she detected a note of wistfulness in his voice.

"James," Rebecca asked him one Sunday evening, "have you found out yet what special work you are supposed to do?"

He did not answer immediately. They were driving along at a leisurely pace on their way to the singing.

"James," Rebecca said again.

"I heard you, Rebecca, but I don't know how to say this," he said.

"Why not?" Becky wondered.

"You might laugh and think it's just my idea. Something I want and maybe not what I'm supposed to do," he finished.

"How will I know unless you tell me? I won't laugh. Really," Becky promised.

"Rebecca, I've felt for some time now that the Lord is calling me to be an evangelist. But now, I wonder, do the Amish have evangelists?" There was so much he did not know about Amish ways.

Rebecca was embarrassed to tell James she did not know what an evangelist was. To be safe, and not expose too much ignorance, she said, "I don't know. You will have to ask my dad. He would know."

David Eash told James that the Amish feel they need their preachers at the home church. "We have our hands full with our own," he said. Then, to prove his point, he remarked, "Just look at what happened with Sam Lapp and Willy and Freeman. We need to work with them, I'd say."

James did not respond. Had he been mistaken then? Was it a desire of his own and not a calling from God?

Now Rebecca understood what an evangelist was. She marveled at the concern James had for other people. It made her feel good.

James was thinking that what David Eash said was true. *But what if Sam and his buddies refuse to listen? Should we then not give others the gospel so they can be saved?*

17
A Farm Visit

The Feltman children were home on a week's vacation. They asked Becky all kinds of questions about life on a farm.

"How many strawberry trees do you have at your house?" Jenny asked Becky.

"They don't grow on trees, Jenny. They grow on plants in the garden."

"Do you get fresh eggs from your roosters every day?" Billy wanted to know.

"If you don't have electricity, how can you watch TV?"

"What's the speed limit for buggies?"

Rebecca laughed at their ignorance, but she also remembered how ignorant she was of the modern appliances in the Feltman home.

So, when Jenny asked her if everything at her house was Amish, Becky decided to find out if she would be allowed to take the children for a weekend visit to her home. She was sure her parents would not mind. She would ask Mrs. Feltman without the children knowing her plan and thus not risk disappointing them.

"I think that would be a fine idea, but are you sure it wouldn't be a bother?" Stella Feltman asked.

"No bother at all. I'd be glad to have them, if they want to come."

There was no question about that. The children were elated. They packed enough clothes for two weeks instead of a weekend. On Friday they kept asking Becky how long it would be before time to go. Becky had obtained her parents' permission to bring the Feltman children along home. Therefore, they were not surprised to see her come with her two charges that Friday afternoon.

Ellie went out to greet them and help carry bags. But Stella Feltman would hear nothing of it.

"It's not necessary for you to carry anything, Mrs. Eash," she said. "My children are to take care of themselves while they are here. No need to make extra work for you." Then admonishing her two children again to remember their manners and listen to Becky, she left.

Billy was ten years old and a regular whirlwind. Jenny was seven and a bit shy, but full of questions.

As soon as Billy saw David, he called him Grandpa.

"Why do you call my dad Grandpa?" Becky asked.

"He just looks like a grandpa, with his long white beard and the pleats in his face. Your mom has them, too. The pleats I mean, not the beard." They laughed.

"Those pleats are called wrinkles," Becky told Billy.

"Can I go find the eggs now?" Billy asked.

Earlier, Rebecca had told him he might be allowed to help gather eggs that evening if her dad hadn't done the chores before they got there.

"Well, pretty soon," David told him. It was easier to go and gather them than to listen to Billy's "Is it time now?"

"Come on, Jackrabbit," said David. "Let's go." And he

picked up the egg basket.

"Me too?" asked Jenny.

"Yes, you too," David said.

"Why do you call me Jackrabbit?" Billy wanted to know.

"Well, you called me Grandpa because of my white beard. I called you Jackrabbit because you hop around. I guess that makes us even," answered David.

"What do you call my sister, then?"

"Oh, she is as shy as a violet, but I think I'll just call her Jenny."

As soon as the door opened, Billy popped inside. He went straight to the nests, where quite a few hens were sitting, and here he learned his first lesson.

"Get out, rooster," he said, and before David could stop him, he reached out his hands to lift the hen off its nest.

"Ouch," he cried. "That rooster tried to eat me!"

David chuckled at the city boy's remark, even though he knew the hens could peck hard and it hurt.

"Let me take the hens off the nests, Jackrabbit, and then you children can get the eggs."

This time Billy was ready to wait.

"Now pick up one egg at a time and put it in my basket. Do it carefully. We don't want to break any."

Jenny was a bit frightened after what had happened to her brother. But very gingerly she reached in and picked up an egg.

"Look how many this one laid," remarked Billy.

"This one too," Jenny said.

Mr. Eash explained that the ones that laid the eggs were the hens and that many hens sat on the same nests in one day. "Each hen only lays one egg a day. Some only lay every other day."

"What do the roosters do?" asked Billy.

"They crow," David said.

Becky decided she would help with the milking. Since

the *Dawdy Haus* had been rented out, the barn now contained two cows instead of just one, to provide milk for the renters.

Billy ran excitedly ahead of Becky and his sister with that half hop in his stride.

"Are your cows Amish, too?" asked Jenny.

"No, they are just cows," laughed Becky.

The children had never watched anyone milk cows before. In fact, they had never been on a farm before.

"How do you do that, Becky? How do you make the milk come?" Billy asked.

"Just watch," Becky answered as she kept milking. Jenny liked the sound of the ping-ping the milk made as it filled the pail.

"Can I try?" Billy begged.

"All right, if you are sure you want to," Becky said.

Billy tried and tried, but to no avail. Not one drop could he produce.

"She's empty, Becky," he exclaimed.

"No, she still has milk," answered the amused girl. "Here, first you squeeze, then you pull. Watch," Becky showed him again.

Finally, he was able to get one short stream. He was as proud as if he had just milked a whole barn full of cows.

"I did it!" he shouted, "Jenny, did you see? I milked a cow! You try it now." But Jenny had decided she would rather not get close to one of those big animals.

The mother cat came with her four little ones for their evening portion of warm milk.

"Oh look. Here is a cat with little kitties," Jenny told her brother. Quick as a wink, Billy grabbed one of the kittens. It spit in protest, and so he dropped it just as suddenly.

"He growled at me," Billy said to Becky.

"No, dogs growl, cats spit and meow. You must be

gentle with him. If you watch, I will show you a trick," Becky said. She milked a stream from the cow straight into the mother cat's mouth. The cat loved it and lapped it up as fast as Becky milked. How the children laughed.

Suppertime was a new experience for the Feltman children also. They were used to having meat, potatoes, vegetables, and dessert for their evening meal. Tonight they got their first taste of *Brockelsupp* (cold milk soup). It consisted of nice ripe strawberries, sugar, bread, and cold milk. The rest of the menu was fresh garden lettuce and radishes, and, of course, half-moon pie.

Billy liked everything and ate a lot, but Jenny didn't care for the soup. Becky asked if she would like a bowl of strawberries and a bit of cream.

She answered politely, "Yes please." So that's what she ate, and enjoyed every spoonful. She thought to herself how kind and understanding Becky was.

"Why do you and your mother wear those caps on your heads?" Jenny asked Becky.

"Because in the Bible it says a woman should have her head covered when she prays," Becky answered.

"Well, I pray," Jenny said, "and I never wear one of those. Doesn't God hear me if I don't wear a cap?"

"I'm sure he hears all little children," Becky told her little friend. "I've been brought up this way and was taught to wear it."

"Where is your bathroom?" Billy asked.

David told him he would have to go to a little house out back. When the boy returned, he said, "I sure don't like your bathroom. There is no shower or tub there, it doesn't smell good, and you can't even flush it. Yuck!"

Jenny didn't like it any better.

Neither did they care for bathing in a tin tub. But yet, there were so many interesting things to see and do at this Amish home.

"What do you do after your work is done in the evening, Grandpa?" Billy asked David.

"Well now," answered David, "I like to read or sometimes just sit on the swing with Grandma and talk."

"I don't think I'd like that very much," said the little fellow.

"No, I don't suppose you would," David agreed.

"Don't you wish you had a TV set so you could watch a good movie?"

"No, Billy, I don't," David answered quickly. Billy looked at him startled. He couldn't imagine anyone not wanting a TV.

"How would you like to play checkers?" said David.

"I don't know how, but maybe I can learn," answered Billy.

"Well come into the living room, Jackrabbit, and I'll show you."

Billy loved the game and they played quite a while, with David letting him win more than one round.

"Where did you buy this game?" asked Billy, "I'd like to have one."

"I didn't buy it. I made it," Mr. Eash told him. They were using black and white buttons for checkers.

"Could you make me one?" Billy wanted to know. "I could teach my dad how to play, when he has time," he added.

"Sure I could, Jackrabbit, but I think we have played enough. We had better go see what Becky and your sister have been up to."

All this while, Rebecca had been teaching Jenny how to make hollyhock dolls and had shown her the name cards her many friends had given her. Then they looked at stacks of cards and gifts Becky had received when she had been in the hospital.

"Didn't you ever have a real doll, Becky?" Jenny asked.

"No, I never did," she answered.

"Oh, Becky, I have so many. You can have one of mine," her little friend offered.

"That's very kind of you, Jenny, and I do thank you, but I'm too old for dolls."

"Well, if I would have known you when you were little, I would have let you play with my dolls all the time," Jenny said.

The two little visitors were so tired by bedtime that, even though they were at a stranger's house, they slept all through the night. In fact, to his disappointment, Billy slept right through chore time.

After breakfast, Becky announced that it was time to go to church. The children enjoyed the buggy ride and David even permitted Billy to take the reins for a while.

"How fast can your buggy go?" Billy asked.

"Only as fast as my horse can run," David told him.

The two little "English" children thought church would never end. They were tired from sitting on backless benches and listening for three hours to words they could not understand. They were tired of being stared at, not realizing they were doing the same to the little Amish children.

Finally, services were over with. Jenny stayed close to Becky and Billy followed David. They were surprised to eat a meal at the house where church was held. By and by a few of the children, prompted by their parents, invited the city boy and girl to join in some games. The boys played tag. The girls had a good game of drop the handkerchief. Nevertheless, both children were glad when they climbed onto the buggy and started for the Eash home.

"I don't think I want to be Amish after all," Billy said. "I like the farm, but I don't like to sit so long in church."

Becky and her parents just smiled.

18
The Dream

The Rowans were moving out of the *Dawdy Haus*. Mr. Rowan had found work that paid much better. It was in Centerville and he didn't like to drive so far each day. The Eash family hated to see them leave. They had been such good renters. But they were happy for the Rowans and wished them God's blessings.

Now the *Dawdy Haus* would be empty once more. *Perhaps not for long,* Rebecca thought. James had asked her to marry him. She was so happy. James had given up so much for her and she loved him dearly. Maybe they could live in the *Dawdy Haus*.

Rebecca's father had another idea. One Sunday afternoon, when James was visiting with the family in the living room, David said, "James, I would like to talk to you and Rebecca about something that's been on my mind."

Becky's heart skipped a beat. Surely he couldn't object to their marriage. James had conformed to the standards of the Amish church and never once complained.

"What do you want to talk about, Dad?" Becky asked.

She looked so serious that David Eash couldn't help but tease a bit.

"Well, you see," David began, "Mom and I are getting older and we don't know if we can manage without you."

"I've been working away from home for quite a while now," Becky reminded him, "and I didn't hear you or Mom say anything before about this."

David never changed his expression a bit as he continued. "That's true, Becky, but at least you are here on weekends to help Mom do windows and wash walls and other things she can hardly manage."

Even James thought he was serious until David said, "We can't spare Becky—unless you two would consent to live in here so Grandma and I could move in the *Dawdy Haus*," he finished with a grin.

"*Ach*, Dad," Becky said in relief, "you had me scared for a bit. I thought you meant it."

"I was beginning to worry, myself," James confessed.

"You should know your dad well enough by now to know he enjoys playing tricks any chance he has," Ellie reminded her daughter.

"But I never can tell when he means it or if he is just kidding, Mom," said Becky.

"That's the fun of it," David remarked.

"Fun for who?" his daughter asked.

"Really though," Mr. Eash said, "Mom and I are going to have to slow down. I can hardly keep up with this large farm anymore, since the boys are gone. Sure, they have been coming home and helping out whenever they can. Even though we trade work, I've had to hire help the last two summers. That doesn't pay too well, either. And now that the Rowans are moved out of the small house, I'll have less help. Mom and I talked it over and we wonder if you would be interested in living here and taking on the farm."

Rebecca hoped James would say yes. Think of it! She could live in the house she loved so well. On this place called home.

"I don't know a lot about running a farm," James told Becky's father, "but I'm willing to learn."

"No one can ask more than that," David answered. "I have confidence in you."

It was decided then and Becky's heart overflowed with happiness. It was so much like her parents moving home, when her grandmother needed someone to take over the farm. Again history was repeating itself.

"Let's walk down to the pond," Becky said to James. "I love to go down there and sit under the willow tree and meditate."

"And what do you think about down here by yourself?" he asked as they reached the big tree and sat in the shade of its overhanging branches.

"Oh, a lot of things," she answered.

"Ever about me?" James said.

"*Ach*, of course I do, you know that," she told him.

"Guess I just wanted to hear you say it. I hope it's all good things," James commented.

"Naturally. Why wouldn't it be? Oh, sometimes I wonder if you are really happy that you are now Amish. Are you, James?" She needed to be reassured.

"Whatever makes you happy, makes me happy too," he answered. But that was not what she wanted to hear.

"James, that is not what I asked you," Becky said. "Please answer me."

"Rebecca, don't," he said, turning away for a moment. He did not even want to admit to himself that it was a very hard transition for him to make. "Becky," James said looking at her with tears in his eyes, "I must tell you about a dream I had. It seems it had a message for me that I had better heed."

"What is it, James?" she asked.

"I dreamed that I'm to be an evangelist and do much speaking. This would mean a lot of traveling. I could not be of much help on this farm, and I don't believe I can learn the German language well enough to preach in the Amish church."

"Oh, James, what will we do?"

"I don't know, Rebecca," he answered. "It might be best if we just break up and I go back to the church I grew up in."

Becky couldn't speak, for her voice would end in sobs if she tried.

"I should never have tried making the change," James said. "I thought it would work and I'd be happy and so would you, but that dream keeps coming back. I can't even tell you all about it now. It was as if I were on holy ground. Rebecca, I must go back. I cannot fight against this calling."

"Then I shall go with you," Rebecca said.

"Are you sure?" asked James.

"Yes, I am, James," she answered without a bit of hesitation.

How glad he was to hear those words.

"What about your family, Becky? Won't they turn against you?"

"Not if they really love me. Besides, I've already experienced God's love among Mennonites, and I'm sure that in their church I can seek to please God."

"Yes, Becky, we do need the fellowship and counsel of those of like faith. Amish and Mennonites have the same basic beliefs and try to obey God and live for peace, but sometimes in different ways. With the Mennonites we may be able to share the gospel widely—as I feel God called me to do in the dream."

After a time James took Becky's hands in his larger

ones and said, "Let's pray together that the Lord may lead us and bless us both in his service."

So there, by the side of the lake under the willow, the two young people bowed in sacred communion with their Maker. This became a hallowed place to them and many times in their daily tasks, as they looked toward this spot, they were reminded of their talk with God.

"Well, I guess I'll go tell your parents of our decision," James told Becky. "I hope I can break it to them gently. They will be disappointed with me, and for that, I'm sorry."

"We will both go and tell them, James," Rebecca decided. "It was your plan to return to the Mennonite Church, but it was my choice to go with you, remember?"

So, hand in hand, they started toward the house.

Rebecca was surprised how calm she was. She had fully expected to be very nervous. When they reached the house, her parents were sitting on the porch swing.

"We thought maybe you two ran away," David said, "you were gone so long."

"Pull those chairs over on the north side, Becky," her mother told her. "The sun won't shine on you there."

Obediently, James helped Rebecca and they placed the chairs close to the swing. As soon as they were seated, they both began to talk.

"Whoa, wait a minute," said David. "One at a time. You sure must be excited to tell us something."

"It is not going to be easy to tell you," James told David, "but I feel I should be the one."

He looked so concerned that both Mr. Eash and his wife were alarmed. What could it be?

"*Yah well,*" David said, "*Was is letz* (what is wrong)?"

"I have decided to go back to my people and the Mennonite church."

Before Becky's parents could comment on this, their

daughter said, "And I'm going with him."

At first, David and Ellie just sat in silence. Then Becky's mother spoke.

"What happened? What went wrong, Becky?"

"Nothing went wrong, Mom. It's just that. . . ."

James interrupted. "I'll explain it, Becky," he said. "First of all, I deeply appreciate the Amish church taking me in. I want you to know that. I think very highly of your people. Although I was not enthusiastic about some of the practices, yet I was determined to cooperate. And I felt certain I could make myself at home among your group.

"However, I've been given a message in a dream which I cannot share completely at this time. Not even with Rebecca. But the Lord has made plain to me what I must do with my own life. I cannot do it if I remain Amish because your church would not allow it. I would be working with non-Amish and sometimes even non-Mennonite people. Although I very much wanted to share a life here with you and your daughter, I must obey God even above my own desires. I will release your daughter from her promise to marry me, if she wants to remain with her own church," James finished. Tears were streaming down his face.

Turning to her parents, Rebecca informed them that it had been her own decision to go with James to his Mennonite way of life. "James did not ask me to leave the Amish. It is my choice. I do not see that much difference. We believe in the same God and that Jesus is his Son. We both believe in the gospel of peace, and we help each other. The difference is in things and I'm not that concerned about things. They shall pass away. But like Ruth of old, where James goes, I will go; where he lives, there I shall live; his people shall be my people and his God, my God." She too was crying by the time she finished talking.

Becky's mother also was wiping tears from her face.

Then David voiced his opinion. "We had always hoped to keep our children within the fold. There are going to be problems in the church, but you have to live your own lives. Just be sure you live them for the Lord. Shun all evil and worldly temptations. Be obedient and faithful members if you choose to go to the Mennonite church. Love your neighbor and keep the commandments," he advised them.

Both James and Rebecca acknowledged that is what they aimed to do.

"I guess that means you will need to look to one of the other children for help with the farm and to move home," Becky told her dad.

How surprised she was to hear him say, "Not necessarily, Rebecca. We will think about it, but I don't know why you couldn't live here if James agrees."

James did agree. But this was not so with some of Becky's brothers and sisters. In fact, some of them were very outspoken with their opinions.

"It just isn't right," voiced her sister, Anna. "If Becky is leaving the church, she won't be satisfied living in this house without electricity or a telephone and all those other worldly things. Once she is Mennonite, she can have them, you know. I didn't think it was a good idea to let her work for the English people in town."

Her brother Roy also expressed himself in no uncertain terms. "James had this in his mind all along. He had no intentions of staying Amish. The church should never have taken him in. I'm surprised you didn't see right through him, Dad," he commented.

David felt much worse at the attitude his children were taking than he did about James and Rebecca. He and Ellie prayed much for wisdom in the matter. One evening he called all his children home.

"Let us not be divided in this," he pleaded. "James and Rebecca have not denied their faith in God. What does the Bible tell us we must do to be saved? Our wish was to have you all remain Amish, and I want you to know we are truly grateful for each who did. Nevertheless, Rebecca is still our daughter and we will treat her as such."

Rebecca loved him more at that moment than ever before.

19
Changing Church Membership

Rebecca's true friends stood by her. Even though they hated to see her leave the Amish and their Sunday evening singings, they told her they wished her well. There were others who judged her harshly.

"You are just leaving so you can have all those worldly things and dress fancy," Katie Zook told her.

"Don't say that, Katie, please don't. It isn't true. Sure I'll use the more convenient things, and even dress as Mennonites do, but that isn't why I'm going," Becky told her sincerely.

"Oh yeah, why are you changing then?" asked Katie's friend Gertie.

"Because I feel my place is to go with James. I have prayed a lot about this and I feel God is leading me," Becky answered.

"Humph," snorted Katie. "I'd say James is the one doing the leading. We can make ourselves believe anything."

"I'm sorry you feel this way," Becky told the two girls. "I'd like to stay friends."

"We are not to be friends with those who break their vows to the church," Gertie reminded her.

"When I was baptized I made my vows to God in front of the church. I did say I would be a faithful member and I've tried to be faithful all along. I intend to do the same in the Mennonite church I will belong to from now on."

"Come on, Gertie," Katie said, "Let's go. We can't do anything with her. She will do as she pleases. Just remember you are making your bed, so don't complain when you have to lie in it." They were gone.

"Don't mind them, Becky," her friend, Anna, told her. Several other girls had been in the room and heard Gertie and Katie. It made them sad that anyone would speak so unkindly. "We sure don't feel that way," they assured Becky.

Rebecca was almost glad it was her last Sunday attending Amish church. It was known that she was leaving. Deacon Amos would come talk with her again, and she didn't have long to wait. Early Monday morning, before she left for work at the Feltman's, he came.

"Rebecca," he said to her on the front porch, "I wish I wouldn't have to tell you this, but the other ministers sent me to inform you that the church is excommunicating you unless you confess your wrong."

"I know," Becky answered, "but I am not doing wrong as I understand God's word."

"I hate to see you leave," Amos said. "We have a fine group of young people and you were one of them. We need you to help build up the church. Maybe if James would just try a little longer, he would learn to speak the language. Others have," the deacon concluded.

"It isn't the German, Amos. That's not why he isn't staying Amish."

"What is it, then?" he asked. "Rebecca, I hope it isn't for the car and other things he had."

"No, I assure you, it isn't," she told him.

"*Well, was dann* (well, what is it then)?" Amos Byler asked again.

"I can't tell you everything, but he had a dream and he said he must do what he was told to do."

"And what's that?" Amos questioned further.

"I don't know other than he said he has a call to be an evangelist," Becky answered.

"You are sure you won't change your mind, then?"

"I'm sure," was her reply.

"So be it. I've done my part and now I'll have to bring this before the church. I'm sorry to have to deal with you in this way. Sam Lapp will also be put in the ban next church Sunday. He will not put away his car and obey church rules. Lately, he has been picked up again for drinking and stealing. He and two Mennonite boys."

"I'm real sorry to hear that." Rebecca meant it.

"I just want to tell you yet," Deacon Byler said, "how much I appreciated you staying in the *Ordnung* (discipline, standards) of the church while you were a member. Other than going with a boy from another congregation, you were never disobedient." Then he added, "Wherever you go, keep your faith and trust in God and be obedient."

She saw tears in the dear old man's eyes and Becky had some of her own to brush away. Why did he make it so hard for her? If he had scolded Becky, it would have been easier. *Maybe*, she thought, *I'm closer to our people than I knew.*

"Oh, I called them our people," she said to herself. She did not quite realize it until she had said it. Now she understood better that a bond had been formed between her and her church home. Worshiping, living, and working together had made her who she was. Breaking with her church family was harder than she had expected.

For some time she had been driving to work with Susan. They both went at the same time on Monday morning and came home Friday afternoon. This worked out well for them, as it did for their employers also.

Not more than fifteen minutes after Amos left, she heard Susan drive up to the front gate.

"I'll see you Friday night, Mom," Becky said, picking up her small suitcase. "If none of the girls come home this week, just leave the window washing for me. I'll do it Friday evening or Saturday."

As she went out the door, Ellie thought, *Why can't she be satisfied to stay Amish like we are? She is such a helpful girl. She is always thinking of others first.*

"Susan," Becky asked as soon as they had said their hellos, "did James tell you he is coming back to your church and I'm coming with him?"

"No, he didn't, Becky. He didn't say a word to me, but then I hardly saw him all weekend. I'm so glad, Becky. Just think, we'll see each other every Sunday. But what did your parents say?" Susan asked all out of breath.

"You sure do rattle on, Susan," Becky told her, laughing happily.

"I can't help it. I'm so excited. Come on, tell me more," coaxed her friend.

"My parents would like for me to stay Amish, naturally. But they accept my decision. One of my brothers and my sister Anna are not very happy with me. My dad asked if James and I would consent to move on my home place and— "

But that's as far as she got when Susan interrupted with a squeal of delight, "That would be simply wonderful, Becky. Oh, just think, we would still be neighbors. I just can't believe how everything is working out."

"Susan, calm down," Becky said. "You are driving and pretty soon you will forget about that and land us in the ditch." She laughed at Susan's enthusiasm as she spoke.

"I'm glad you told me, Becky. This will make my week so much brighter. I dreaded coming to work because of a problem with a couple of our boys and if it's on the news, I'm sure my boss and his wife will question me about it."

"You mean the Kalp and Damon boys?" Becky asked.

"Yes, those are the ones. They were caught drinking and stealing," Susan told her.

"I know. Sam Lapp was in on it too."

"Why do they do such foolish things, anyway?" Susan wondered.

"I don't know," Becky answered. "Some people from our church say it's not such a bad thing. They are just sowing their wild oats. Once they get married, they will settle down."

"You surely don't agree with that, do you, Becky?"

"Of course not. If they only settle down so they can marry, that's the wrong reason. Besides, if I were a girl who dated them, I'd hate to take that chance."

"Yeah, me too," Susan agreed. "They don't always settle down. We have a case in our church just like that. Soon after the couple married, the husband went back to drinking. He had promised faithfully he never would. Eventually they had a family of little children. He couldn't hold a job long, so to feed his hungry family, he began to steal."

"What happened to them, Susan?" Becky asked.

"He is in jail right now and our church family helps her. She does some day work at places where she can take her youngest child along. It's real sad."

"Here we are already," Becky said. "Don't bother pulling up the driveway. I'll walk up. Thanks, and call me if you aren't busy," Becky told Susan.

With a wave of her hand, Susan called out, "I will," and drove away.

Rebecca started out with her usual tasks as she did every Monday morning at the doctor's house.

First she sorted the clothes and started the laundry. What a difference it was from doing the washing at Mony Lapp's, as she had several summers before. Next, she rinsed all the dirty dishes left from the weekend and put them in the dishwasher. Now to pick up the newspaper scattered all over the living room. Then she saw it.

In big bold letters on the front page it read "Amish and Mennonite Boys Jailed in Local Robbery." Becky read on. The whole shameful story was there for everyone to read. She was thankful, however, that the reporter was kind enough to print the fact that such behavior is not condoned by either church.

On Wednesday afternoon, Susan called Becky.

"Did you see the newspaper?" she asked.

"Yes, I saw Sunday's soon after I got here," Becky told her.

"No, I mean today's!" Susan said.

"I didn't bring it in yet. Why?" Becky asked.

"Well, just go get it and read the front page, then call me back."

"All right," Becky said. She knew by the sound of Susan's voice that something was wrong. In a way, she dreaded finding out.

Reluctantly, she took the paper and looked in unbelief at what she read. "Three Desperadoes make Jailbreak." It went on to say it was suspected some files or small saws had been smuggled in by other young folks who came to visit the evening before. What a disgrace. The boys had not been found yet, but a statewide search was under way. Rebecca did not know the parents of two of the boys, but her heart went out to them as well as to Emmanuel and Amanda Lapp. She knew they didn't want their boys to be wayward sons.

After she composed herself a bit, she called Susan.

"Isn't it just awful?" Susan said, "Have the Feltman's talked to you about it?" she asked.

"Yes, they did a little bit the first evening, but I think they know I feel bad about it, so they haven't said too much."

"Well, mine sure did. Especially Mr. Max. He seems to think it's a big joke. What could I do, Rebecca, to let him know we don't think it's funny?" Susan asked her friend.

Becky was surprised. Here was the girl she always felt was so much wiser than she, and now Susan was asking advice. What should she say?

"Susan, maybe if you told him how bad you feel about it, he would not heckle you anymore," Becky said helpfully.

"Perhaps that would make a difference. I'm going to try."

They talked for a short while about James and his decision.

"He was so quiet for a few weeks," Susan said. "I was afraid maybe you two had a disagreement and were about to split up."

"Oh, no, Susan, but I think James has been doing a lot of serious thinking."

"Have you and he set a wedding date yet?" Susan asked.

"A wedding date?" Becky exclaimed in mock surprise. Then she realized how silly she was to fake innocence. Susan knew he had asked her to marry. So she answered truthfully, "No, Susan, we haven't, but I'm sure when we do, you will be one of the first I'll tell."

"Good," she answered, "I hope it's soon."

Susan had a secret of her own, but she wanted just the right time and place to tell her best friend. So it must wait until another day.

151

20
Engaged

James came over on Saturday night. He didn't know if he would be welcomed by Becky's parents as he was before, but he felt just as much at home with them as when he was Amish. They talked of many things. Sam and the other two jailbreakers had been caught and their sentences extended. Everyone was hoping that through this experience they would decide to mend their ways.

Then David said, "Are you still willing to move here on the farm and take over for me?"

"If you trust me with it," James replied, "and if I can speak English to your animals. I don't believe they understand my Dutch too well."

"Oh, they understand the language pretty good, but I don't think my chickens appreciate a whole horse in their water fountain," David reminded him, and they laughed together.

James invited Rebecca to go along to church and then to his house afterwards for lunch.

"Are you sure it's all right with your mother?" Becky

asked. "I don't want to be a bother."

"You couldn't be a bother if you tried," James told her. "Besides, I've already asked my mother if you can come and she said she would be happy if you would accept."

"I'll be happy to come," Becky told James, to his delight.

He had not sold his horse and buggy yet, so when Sunday morning came, James came for her with the rig. He informed Becky they were going to his home where Arnie Johns would take them along to church.

"He is coming by for Susan anyway and told me he would be more than glad to have us accompany them. Becky noticed that James had his regular haircut and was wearing the suit that he wore when first they met, what some Amish would call an English style.

"Today we shall both be excommunicated from the church I've attended all my life," Becky remarked as they drove along.

"Are you sorry about that?" James asked her.

"I'm only sorry that we can't all go on being friends," she answered. "Most of us will stay as we were, but some will shun me."

"Rebecca, in all areas of life there are people who will avoid your company if you disagree with them. Not only in church-related matters. You will still have fellowship with God and a new group of Christians. That's the most important part."

"You are right, James," she agreed. "It's just that I like to be on good terms with everyone."

"That's your nature, and a true Christian desires it to be so. I appreciate your attitude, but we just can't please everyone."

"I know. I've been told that before."

They rounded a bend in the road approaching the Kauffman place. The Levi Kauffman family was just coming out of their driveway from behind a row of evergreen trees. The two buggies almost collided. Levi reined his horse in sharply as James made a quick swerve to the left. Both drivers stopped. You could plainly see that Mrs. Kauffman was shaken up. She was holding baby Joni on her lap, and upon the near impact she had tightened her grip on him so fiercely that he was protesting loudly.

"Why does he yell so?" asked eight-year-old Laura.

"*Ach*," answered her Mom, "I *drickted* (squeezed) him too hard."

"I'm really sorry, Levi," James called out. "I didn't see you because of the curve. Is everyone all right?"

"We are all right, James. We just got a good jolting, that's all. That curve and the trees are a real nuisance."

"I'm glad no one got hurt," James said.

"We are sure sorry to lose you two," Levi ventured to tell them. "Hope it isn't anything we did or said."

"I assure you and your wife both, it isn't. It was our own decision. I hope we can still be friends," James said.

"Why couldn't we be?" Levi asked. "You and Becky just be faithful in serving God and don't follow the fashions of the world," he advised.

"That's the way we want to live," James answered. His horse was impatient and prancing to go. So they bade each other good-bye and went on their separate ways—the Kauffman's to worship God with their Amish church and way and James and Rebecca to their worship of the same God in their Mennonite church and way.

How wonderful, thought Rebecca. *God is everywhere. He understands all languages. He knows the hearts of all people. How great he is!*

Neither she nor James had spoken for a little while. Suddenly, Becky began to laugh.

"What are you laughing about?" James asked. "What's so funny?"

"It just struck me how different it looks to see you and me driving in this buggy," she said.

"Really," James remarked, "we've done it before."

"Yes, but not dressed like this. I'm wearing my Amish garb yet and you are dressed English."

They both laughed. "It does look rather strange, I suppose. But to me, it proves again we don't have to be alike to get along."

Arnie and Susan were ready and waiting when James turned into the Miller driveway.

"Where have you two been?" asked Mr. Miller. "We thought you might have lost your way," he joked.

Apologetically, James explained the situation that took place at Levi Kauffman's place.

"We're just thankful no one was hurt and you got here in time for church, if we hurry," Mrs. Miller added.

The Millers left immediately, telling the young folks not to be late.

Becky had never been to James's church before.

"Oh, Susan," she worried, "I don't know where to sit or how I'm to do."

"Don't worry, Becky. You'll sit with me and my friends this morning. I don't suppose our way of worship is much different from what you are used to. We have singing, praying, and preaching same as you did, except in English. I'll be with you all the time, but tonight I'll be with Arnie and you can sit with James," she said, winking at her brother.

"In church?" remarked Becky in surprise.

"Are you ashamed to sit by me in church?" James asked in mock amazement.

"Of course not," Becky answered. "It's just that men and women never sit together in Amish services, except at funerals."

"Well, tonight you have my permission to sit with me,

if you care to," James told her.

Susan was true to her promise. She and Becky sat together through both Sunday school and church service. Becky knew quite a few of the other girls from meeting them at the literary meetings. But she did not know the Sunday school teacher who stood in front of the all-girls' class.

The teacher asked Susan who her visitor was. Then she welcomed Rebecca and introduced herself.

"I am Joy Lehman," she said. "We are glad you are with us today. Do you have a quarterly?"

Rebecca was embarrassed. She did not know what a quarterly was.

Susan quickly put her at ease by saying, "I'll share mine with her."

"Thank you, Susan," said Mrs. Lehman.

"This is my Sunday school lesson book," Susan explained, offering it to Becky. How glad Rebecca was for a friend like Susan. She was also impressed with Joy Lehman and her teaching. In the Amish church women do not speak or take leading parts, so here was something else foreign to her.

Today's lesson was about the five wise and five foolish virgins. The story was familiar to Becky, but Joy made it so real. She listened with rapt attention. The sermon that followed was just as soul-stirring. Instead of three or four ministers, as Becky was used to at preaching services, there was only one. She wondered about this. *How can one man take upon himself such an awesome responsibility?* she thought.

The sermon was about forgiveness. She saw and felt the sincerity of the minister as tears ran down his cheeks. Becky couldn't believe it when the services closed. It was only eleven-thirty, yet she felt spiritually filled.

156

"Why do you only have one minister?" Becky asked soon after they started back to Susan's house. "How can he take care of such a big church by himself?"

"We have elders in the church to help him and there has been some talk of ordaining another minister," James informed her.

"Yeah," Arnie said, "and I think James might be the man."

James was silent, but Becky saw that mysterious expression she noticed when he had told her part of his dream.

Susan broke the silence by saying, "Becky, Arnie is staying for lunch, too. I'm glad it's such a nice day because it's special."

Becky thought, too, it was an exceptional day. Only one thing cast a shadow for her. She thought of her parents, brothers, and sisters, perhaps at this very moment hearing the words of her excommunication. She knew there would be tears. Life was full of joys, heartaches, and sorrows and she realized that none can escape them.

Soon, though, she was caught up in the happiness around her.

What a meal they had. The table was set with Orpha Miller's best dishes. A big platter of nicely browned chicken was in the center, surrounded by mounds of creamy mashed potatoes, gravy, corn, two kinds of cheese, macaroni salad, graham cracker pudding, and glasses of sparkling lemonade.

Just as everyone was ready to be seated, Susan said, "Before we start eating, Dad, I want to tell you something."

"Can we have our blessing first?" asked Leroy Miller. "Honest, Susan, you are as fidgety as a young colt. The way you jump around here, it must be pretty important."

"It is," she giggled.

157

"Well, let's sit down once," Leroy said.

Orpha assigned each one to a place and they joined hands and hearts in asking a blessing on the food. As soon as the Amen was spoken, Susan arose from her chair.

"My goodness, Susan," her mother remarked, "what's wrong with you?"

"This is the right time and place for my secret, our secret," she corrected herself, looking at Becky first. Then turning to Arnie, she asked him to stand by her side. "Mom, Dad, everyone," she said, "Arnie has asked me to marry him. We are engaged."

"That is, if it's all right with you and Orpha," Arnie addressed Susan's father.

"Well now, I don't know about this," Leroy began. "Don't you think you are a bit young, Susan?"

"Oh, Dad," she said, "you're teasing, aren't you?"

"Of course he is," answered his wife, "and if he keeps it up much longer, the food will get cold." Susan and the others detected a tremor in Orpha's voice and knew, even though she was happy, it was hard to let go. They had good fellowship around the table and a merry time.

Becky didn't know what engaged meant. She would ask Susan later.

"Oh, engaged means when you promise to marry someone, then you are engaged to that person. You will not go with anyone else."

"Then I'm engaged too, Susan," Becky said. "When I was Amish, I would just date for so long until James asked me to go steady with him. But now you and I are both engaged." It sounded very impressive to Becky.

"Just think, Rebecca," Susan said, "we will be sisters-in-law. I don't know anyone I'd rather have for a sister."

"Me too," Becky said, and she felt a kinship to Susan that she had never felt before.

158

21
Becky's Wedding

"How long will you be working for your people?" Becky asked Susan one day.

"I'm not sure. Probably about a year and a half. Why do you ask?"

"I just wanted to make sure I'll have a ride into town to the Feltman's," Becky answered. "James and I have set our wedding date for the fourteenth of February. I suppose I'll only work for the doctor and his wife until New Year's Day."

"Oh, Becky, I am so happy for you. I wish Arnie and I could get married that soon, but I think we have to wait until he is finished with his schooling."

"Well," said Rebecca, "my Dad needs us on the farm by next spring at least. Has James said anything to you or your family if he likes farming?"

"He loves farming," Susan assured her. "He is a good carpenter, but farming is his first choice."

That put Rebecca's mind at ease. Rebecca had wondered if perhaps James consented to run the Eash farm to please her father. Susan's word removed all doubt.

Preparations would need to be made for the wedding. Rebecca had been taken into the Mennonite church as a member, so she changed to the Mennonite way of dressing. No longer did she need to wear pleated coverings or dresses fastened with straight pins. She could even wear printed dresses, but she stayed away from gaudy colors and always dressed modestly.

As is the custom among the Amish, Becky's mother decided she must make a quilt and invited her daughter's friends for a quilting bee. She knew Rebecca's favorite was the double wedding ring pattern. Although the Amish do not wear wedding bands, they will use such a pattern in homemade articles that serve useful purposes. Plans were made to have the gathering the third Tuesday in January. Becky would be finished working in town by then.

Mrs. Feltman and her husband were sorry to lose such a good hired girl. The two Feltman children were just as reluctant.

"But who will clean our house and cook for us?" Jenny asked.

"Oh, Jenny, I'm sure your mother will find someone," Rebecca told her.

"But we don't want someone," Billy complained. "We want you."

"Do you suppose you could find another Amish girl to work for me, Rebecca?" Mrs. Feltman asked.

"All I can say is, I'll try," Becky replied.

"Well, I'm not going to like her anyway!" Billy decided.

"Neither am I," his sister also predicted.

"How do you know you won't?" Becky inquired of the children.

"Cause," was the answer.

"Cause why?" Becky further pursued their reply.

"Cause she won't be nice like you are," Billy told her.

"Oh, she could be much nicer," Becky said. But she had not convinced them. They were impossible the next two weeks. It seemed as if they were different children from those she had known before.

Rebecca heard that Lula Zook wanted work, so she had James take her over to talk with her one Saturday evening. Lula was one of the girls who remained a good friend and she was delighted to see Becky.

"Come in," she invited her. Then, noticing James sitting in the car, she said, "Tell James he is welcome to come in too."

"Thank you, Lula," Becky said, "but we can't stay. I told James I wouldn't be long." Lula wondered what brought her over. She didn't need to wait to find out.

Right away Becky said, "I'm quitting my place in town and the doctor's wife wondered if I could find someone to work for her. I heard you were looking for a regular job. So I came to see if you would be interested."

Lula was elated. "Oh, Becky," she exclaimed, "this is just what I've been looking for. Are they good people to work for?" she asked.

"The best," Becky told her. "They have two children, a boy and a girl, still in grade school. They are usually well-behaved. The pay is good, too. How soon could you start?" Becky asked.

"Right away, Monday morning, if they want me that soon," Lula answered.

"That will work out real well. I will stay a week to break you in, as Mrs. Feltman asked me to. They will pick you up Monday mornings and bring you home Friday afternoons. The wages are forty dollars a week."

"Forty!" Lula was flabbergasted. Never had she dreamed of making so much in one week. *No wonder*, she thought, *Becky was able to buy some good furniture and have a little nest egg besides,* as she had told some of her best friends.

"Oh, I sure want the job, Becky," Lula told her.

"Well then, I'll see you Monday morning. Be ready by eight o'clock."

"Is she going to work for the Feltman's?" James asked, after they had started on their way again.

"Yes," Becky said. "She is so excited about it. She can hardly wait for Monday to come."

The two Feltman children, however, were not so pleased. They scowled at Lula the minute they met her. Stella Feltman tried to reason with her offspring, but as soon as she was gone, they became unmanageable. Several times they even defied Becky and they took no instructions at all from the new maid. When they told Lula she was not their boss and stuck their tongues out at her, Rebecca sent them to their rooms. You could tell they were still rebelling by the sounds coming from upstairs.

"What they need," said Becky, "is a good *Bletsching* (spanking). But I've never given them any and I don't know if the doctor and his wife would allow it."

"They just don't want you to leave," answered Lula. "Give them some time, Becky. I know I can't be you, but maybe after a while, they will accept me. I think so."

That evening at the dinner table, Billy pushed his dessert away because Lula served it instead of his usual *Maut.* He pushed it harder than he intended and it fell upside-down on the floor. Doctor Feltman arose from the table, took his son by the arm, and led him into the den. The two maids soon found out that the doctor did believe in spanking. By Billy's cries of protest, they guessed that an English paddling hurts the same as an Amish *Bletsching.*

Whether it was out of fear of punishment or the talk

Doctor Feltman had with his son, Billy showed respect from that time on. His sister profited from the episode, also, and true to Lula's prediction, it was only a matter of weeks until things were running smoothly. The children never forgot Becky, but they learned you can like more than one hired girl.

The day for the quilting bee had arrived. Every available place around the quilt had been taken. Those who could not find a spot to quilt helped Ellie prepare the noon meal. The girls were busy as a hive of bees. David Eash said they were as noisy as bees, too.

"I believe I'll go outside where there is space to breathe and where my ears won't ring so," he teased. The girls didn't mind him at all. Such remarks were expected from men when quilters were at work. Even though the girls worked long and steadily, the quilt was not completed by evening. Becky wasn't disappointed, for she knew her sisters also wanted to put some of their work into it.

Therefore, it was decided to have a second quilting the next day. Becky took the rig after supper and drove to Annie's house, then to the places of her two brothers and her sister, who lived on the other side of road twenty. She couldn't contact them all that evening, but those she did invite said they would see that the rest of them would be notified. Most of them were able to come, for which Becky was grateful. She didn't care as much about finishing the project as she enjoyed the fellowship with family.

They all seemed to have a good time and were so engrossed in their work and conversation that they could hardly believe it when they were called to lunch. Becky had been seated next to her sister Fannie. When she tried to leave the quilt, she felt something pulling on the skirt of her dress.

"What's this?" Becky said, turning to see why she couldn't walk away from the quilt. The women all began to laugh. Becky had fallen prey to an old Amish trick. While Rebecca was busily visiting and working, Fannie had stitched the hem of her dress to the quilt.

"You are already hooked, Becky," Annie told her. "James can't have you." What fun they had.

"Oh, you women," Becky said, undoing the thread that kept her captive. But she was glad they could have such fun together. By evening, her quilt was finished and it was lovely indeed.

Now it was time for more wedding preparations. She had informed her parents she did not want such a big wedding as her brothers and sisters had.

"It is not necessary," she told them. "I don't want to put you through all that work."

"We did it for the other children," David said, "and we will do it for you too." Her mother agreed also.

"I know you would, Dad," Becky replied, "but James and I would rather just keep it very simple. Besides, there is too much expense for just one day," she finished.

"You won't hear us complain about expense," her father said.

"I know I wouldn't," she agreed with him, "but this is the way we want it to be."

"Very well then," David said. "After all, it is your wedding."

"Surely you will let us have a dinner for you," Ellie remarked.

"Yes, we would appreciate that, but only one meal and not three." The Amish usually had a meal at noon, at evening, and again at midnight for the young folks and others who preferred to stay. So it was decided. Becky's sisters came to help with preparations also.

The meal would be served at Becky's home after the ceremony. Naturally, Ellie wanted everything spick-and-span.

One day when Roy's wife came to help, she brought her child along. The little girl was helping Becky put clear paper doilies in the china cabinet, when she remarked, "My mom said she hopes you won't go so fancy now that you aren't Amish." The remark took Becky by surprise. She thought since her father's talk with his children, everything was going well. Evidently there were some feelings she hadn't known about. She answered the little girl that she had no intentions of going fancy.

Her wedding day was sunny. Many of her Amish relatives and friends came to witness her marriage and help celebrate this special day. James had a car again and came for Rebecca an hour before time for the service to begin. They were to meet with the minister, and they also wanted some time with their attendants, as well as a few minutes alone.

Amish girls always wear blue when they marry. Rebecca wished to wear a white dress, but out of respect to her family and so she wouldn't appear to have gone fancy, she wore blue. James thought she looked absolutely beautiful.

"Oh, Becky," Susan told her, "you and James look so happy. I can't wait until my wedding day. I'm glad I'm one of your attendants. And I hope we always live close and never get too busy to spend time together. Is it scary to get married, Becky?" Susan asked.

"*Ach*, Susan, will you quit? Pretty soon you will have me crying and I don't want to get married with my face all wet," she laughed.

Becky did cry as she spoke her vows and James also shed a few tears. This was such a holy occasion. But nothing touched Rebecca as much as when they opened their gifts and among them was a lovely homemade receipt holder from Deacon Amos Byler, with a note that simply read, "Rebecca, Live for the Lord, Amos Byler." As an afterthought, these words were added: "I hold no ill will."

Rebecca had not known he was present that day. It was an open wedding. He had not stayed for the reception. Had she been aware of his being there, she surely would have invited him to stay. He had made her day complete.

22

The Dream Unfolds

Rebecca Miller and her husband settled into her home place. It seemed strange to write her name as Miller instead of Eash. But it was stranger yet to be the lady of the house. Her mother had always been the queen of this home. Yet her mother was nearby, and Becky often asked her advice.

Electricity had been put into the big house and James also requested to have a telephone. This was accepted among the local Amish, since James, a Mennonite, was running the farm and David couldn't work it himself.

"If we ever move back in the big house again," David told Ellie, "we will take them out."

Becky learned to drive a car, much to her own surprise. It was often helpful when James needed parts for the farm machinery.

One incident happened, though, that James wouldn't let Becky forget. It was her first attempt at driving. As they approached the end of the driveway, she made no indication of stopping.

"Slow down," James told her. She did what she had done for so many years, pulled hard with her hands, saying, "Whoa, whoa!"

"The brakes, push the brake!" James said in panic.

"Where are they?" she cried. Fortunately, James was able to reach across and take control. The driving lessons were continued in the pasture field until Becky had mastered the art. Many times thereafter, as James sent his wife on an errand with the car, his parting remark was, "Don't forget to say 'Whoa!'" She would turn up her nose and pretend she didn't hear as she drove off.

Susan and Arnie were married the next year and lived only five miles from James and Becky's place. They spent many happy times together.

On one such occasion, as they were in conversation around the dinner table at Arnie's house, Susan said, "I saw Sam Lapp's marriage license in the paper."

"Really!" Becky said in surprise. "Who is he getting married to?"

"Would you believe?" Susan remarked, "Remember Doris Gabert?"

"Yes, wasn't she a neighbor to the people you worked for in town?"

"That's the one. She is such a sweet girl. I just hope he is good to her."

"I wonder what his folks say about this," James said.

"Well, I don't know," Susan replied. "You would think they would just be thankful he has changed his ways."

"I would hope so," Becky agreed.

"What about the other two boys who ran around with him?" Becky asked.

"The last I heard, they were both working out West," Arnie told them.

"I certainly hope they come to their senses, too," Susan said.

Sometime later, Becky came face to face with Sam Lapp. She was just coming out of Jason's Mercantile.

"Hello, Rebecca," he said. She acknowledged the greeting and prepared to go on her way, when he spoke again. "This is my wife, Doris," he remarked.

"Hello, Doris," Becky replied.

"Rebecca," Sam began, "we had our differences and I did a lot of foolish and harmful things. We were so young then. I hope you don't hold any grudges." Becky could tell it was hard for Sam to speak. His wife looked totally bewildered.

"What are you talking about, Sam?" she asked her husband.

"I'll explain later," he told her kindly. *Not only have his looks changed, he certainly has too,* thought Becky.

"Sam," she answered, "some things are best forgotten, and that's what I aim to do."

How light her steps felt as she went on down the street.

Becky's first child was a little girl. She looked so much like her mother, that James said, "We must name her Rebecca."

"Oh, James," said his wife, "I want to name her Susan."

"We have no problem then," he answered, "How do you like Rebecca Sue?" Becky loved the name.

"Rebecca Sue Miller," she repeated it over and over. But before the little miss was a year old, she was Susie to all her kin.

James and his wife were both active members in their little congregation. James was the young men's Sunday school teacher, and they gleaned much from him and his knowledge of God's Word. Therefore, it was no surprise at all that, when preparations were made to choose another minister, he was in the lot. Every member of the church submitted a name. Those with more than three votes were in as a candidate to become a minister. James Miller had the highest number and then Arnie Johns. There were two other young men in the lot with them. No special schooling or training was given. A thorough search and acquaintance with the Bible and submission to the Holy Spirit were the credentials needed.

The minister and the area bishop (overseer) met with the four men, both as a group and also privately. They asked each one if he was willing to accept the office of an associate pastor, should he be chosen. They all answered in the affirmative.

James was very quiet all week prior to the ordination service. Becky knew he was deep in meditation and study. They prayed much together and in private also.

Rebecca began to feel a bit of the responsibility that would be hers, should her husband be the one selected. She tried hard to keep the children quieter. They now numbered three. She would give them extra attention and take them outside in the evenings, so James could be left undisturbed. Of course, Grandma Ellie often took them to the little *Dawdy Haus*, which pleased everyone. What a blessing her parents were.

It was a very special Sunday. There were two visiting ministers to assist. The four men who had been selected were seated on the front bench. After a sermon about the duties of ministers and their wives, the hymn "Have Thine Own Way" was sung. Four Bibles had been placed on a small table at the front of the church. Only one Bible contained a slip of paper placed at a designated page. The four men were asked to step forward and select a Bible. They were seated again. The bishop of that district then stepped forward, received the Bibles one at a time, and opened them to the appointed passage. Arnie Johns was the first to relinquish his Bible. He breathed a sigh of relief as the overseer closed it and laid it aside. The next

Bible was opened and closed, and laid aside with the first.

Two more to search in order to find who God's choice would be. James was next to place his Bible in the bishop's hand. The bishop opened the Bible. Everything was so quiet, Rebecca was afraid people could hear her heart beat. She knew already and she felt James had known too, all week. He sat with bowed head, as he heard the bishop say, "The lot has fallen on our young brother James Miller." He read the verse on the slip of paper: "The lot is cast into the lap; but the whole disposing thereof is of the Lord" (Proverbs 16:33). Then the ministers placed their hands on James and prayed that God would bless and strengthen him for the work that lay ahead.

Becky was crying. Her heart went out to James. He was so young to help lead the church. Yet, she realized, he would be working with their minister who had years of experience. This was a comfort.

Since it was the in-between Sunday for Amish church, Becky's parents had come with James and Becky. It touched them deeply as they witnessed the ordination of their son-in-law.

From that day forward, there was a special bond between them.

On their way home from church, little four-year-old Timothy remarked, "Daddy, I hope you get to be made preacher every Sunday."

"Why?" James asked him.

"So Grandpa comes and I can sit with him. He gave me some wintergreen candy, too. That's why," he said.

James filled his place well in the ministry. Yet there was still a restlessness within him. Becky sensed it at times. She did not pry or question him, but tried to be a good, supportive wife.

Four years after James became a minister of the gospel, he was asked to go with a group of men to deliver several truckloads of grain to a poor country in Central America. Rebecca urged him to go.

"We can get along fine," she told him. "If we need to, we can get one of Roy's boys to help. You know that Dad always wants something to do," she told him.

"Are you trying to get rid of me?" James teased.

"Of course not, James, but I just think you should go. You may never get the chance to see what it's like in other parts of the world." Had she known what the future held for them, she may not have been so eager. The church also added their encouragement and, two weeks later, James Miller was on his way. What an experience! The people were not only in need of food and clothing, but also friendship and understanding.

James knew this was the fulfilling of his dream that God had given him years before. Here were people crowded together in need, begging for help, just as he had seen in his vision. There were a few persons who spoke English well enough to understand and translate so that James could converse with them. They were even hungry for the Word of God. James and his friends prayed together and discussed the long-term missionary opportunity there. Together they sensed God calling James to continue that ministry.

What would Rebecca say? How would her family feel about this? Then as he prayed the answer came: "I have taken care of you up to now and will I not continue to do so?" James Miller was ashamed he had ever doubted.

"What do you think, Rebecca?" he asked, after revealing his feelings to her. "This is what the rest of my dream was that I was never able to tell you. But now I know that God wants me with these people to evangelize and minister to their needs. I should have gone then. Now, it will also mean a sacrifice for you, the children, and our families."

Without a moment's hesitation, Rebecca said the same words she had spoken years before: "James Miller, whither you go, I shall go; whither you lodge, I shall lodge; your people shall be my people and your God, my God. Only now, I should say 'we' and 'our' because I speak for the children also."

How he loved her!

Much preparation had to be made, along with many changes. One of Becky's sisters and her husband would be moving home. They knew it would be hard to say good-bye, especially to dear Grandpa and Grandma Eash.

But as Grandpa said, "We are too old to go, so we send you with our blessing."

Their Mennonite mission board provided some training and orientation for James and Becky. They would take Spanish lessons when they got to the country.

The church held a special commissioning service the Sunday evening before the Millers' were to leave. They asked James and Rebecca to come forward. After giving the charge to James, the dear minister turned to Becky and said, "Be thou as a green olive tree in the house of the Lord." Her heart raced. She had heard those words before, but now they had a special meaning. Oh yes, she would be just that. With God's help, she could stand by James and her family, so they might flourish in the shade of her love.

Every one of Becky's brothers and sisters came to see them off.

The entire Miller family was also present as well as many friends and neighbors. Even Dr. and Mrs. Feltman had come, bringing their now nearly grown children.

Just before boarding the plane, their voices blended in singing "God Be with You Till We Meet Again." A prayer was offered, asking for a safe flight.

"If we never see you again here, we will meet you in

heaven," James said as a last farewell.

As they took off, Rebecca couldn't help but think, *Here I am, a former Amish girl going with my family to a place where the name Amish has never been heard.* As she responded to the many hands waving good-bye, she remembered John's vision of people from all nations gathering before God and praising him for salvation.

Rebecca knew that the blessings of God and family went with them as they left their homeland to share the gospel with persons in Central America. And that was enough.

The Author *(continued from page 175)*

(continued from page 175)

Since the publication of *Ellie,* Mary has had numerous speaking engagements. She is a member of the Ohioana Library Association of Columbus, Ohio.

Mary lives at North Canton, Ohio, and is now retired. She is an active member of the Hartville Mennonite Church, serving on the hospitality committee and teaching an adult Sunday school class.

The loss of her husband has brought many adjustments in Mary's life, but she finds the joy of the Lord is her strength. Her four children, their spouses, her eleven grandchildren, and also the church family are a great support to her.

Mary enjoys quilting, reading, writing, and embroidery work. She appreciates her Christian training. Her hope for this book is that it may be a delight and inspiration to those who read it.

The Author

Mary Christner Borntrager was one of ten children born to Amish parents at Plain City, Ohio.

Her early education was eight grades of public school. Later she attended teacher training institute at Eastern Mennonite College, Harrisonburg, Virginia. For seven years she taught at a Christian day school.

At nineteen she became the wife of John Borntrager. Their home was blessed with four children, Jay, Kathryn (Keim), John, and Geneva (Massie).

After her children were grown, she earned a certificate in Childcare and Youth Social Work from the University of Wisconsin. She then worked with emotionally disturbed children and youth for twelve years.

Mary has written several short stories and poems. Her first book, *Ellie,* was released in April of 1988 by Herald Press. Thirty thousand copies were sold in the first year. *Ellie* has inspired Mary to write this sequel about Rebecca, Ellie's daughter. *(continued on 174)*

ELLIE'S PEOPLE

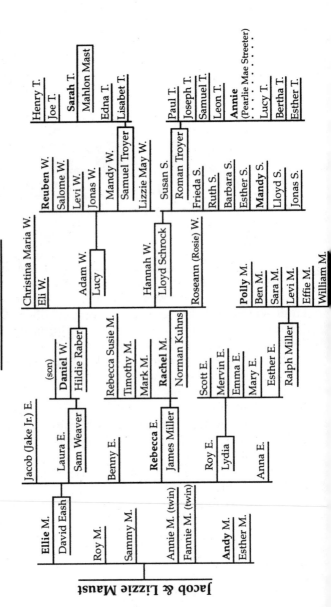

Jacob & Lizzie Maust

Geoff Dyer is the author of three novels: *Paris Trance*, *The Search*, *The Colour of Memory*; a critical study of John Berger, *Ways of Telling*; a collection of essays, *Anglo-English Attitudes*; and three genre-defying titles: *But Beautiful* (winner of a 1992 Somerset Maugham Prize, shortlisted for the *Mail on Sunday/ John Llewellyn Rhys Memorial Prize*), *The Missing of the Somme* and *Out of Sheer Rage* (a finalist for a National Book Critics Circle Award). He is also the editor of *John Berger: Selected Essays* and co-editor, with Margaret Sartor, of *What Was True: The Photographs and Notebooks of William Gedney*. Geoff currently lives in London. His latest book is *Yoga for People Who Can't Be Bothered to Do It*.

'Charming books tend to wither as fashion moves on or as we grow older. *The Catcher in the Rye*, and maybe *Ginger and Pickles*, seem to be exceptions. Then there are books, such as *The Great Gatsby*, whose callowness is itself profound, whose charm is persistingly, enduringly transient. Geoff Dyer has written such a book . . . a book about being thoughtless, young and in love' Candia McWilliam, *New Statesman*

'Four things that get under your skin: shards of glass, splinters of wood, sharp needles, and books by Geoff Dyer. Where most writers barely nick the flesh of human feeling, Dyer somehow manages to dig deeper . . . Unusually for a contemporary English novelist Dyer is as interested in asking big, difficult questions about the meaning of life as he is in developing motifs, displaying his learning, making points, making you laugh, shocking, soothing, or being cool, all of which he manages to do with unnatural ease' *Guardian*

'Compelling . . . A rattling good tale' *The Spectator*

'A vivid, erotic and shocking description of the tragic consequences of intimacy coming to an end . . . brimming with Dyer's usual themes of love, friendship, sex and emotional breakdown' *Mixmag*

'Delightful . . . astonishing' *Mail on Sunday*

PARIS TRANCE

GEOFF DYER

An *Abacus* Book

First published in Great Britain by Abacus in 1998
This edition published by Abacus in 1999
Reprinted 2003

A CIP catalogue record for this book
is available from the British Library.

ISBN 0 349 11204 5

A few pages from this book first appeared, in slightly different form, in
A *Book of Two Halves*, edited by Nicholas Royle (Gollancz, 1996).

Grateful acknowledgement is made to D. M. Conseil for their
kind permission to reprint the lines from 'Nouveau Western'
by MC Solaar, from the album *Prose Combat* (Polydor).

Typeset in Goudy by M Rules
Printed and bound in Great Britain by
Clays Ltd, St Ives plc.

Abacus
An imprint of
Time Warner Books UK
Brettenham House
Lancaster Place
London WC2E 7EN

www.TimeWarnerBooks.co.uk